THE INNER TEMPLE

THE INNER TEMPLE

Kelly Barker

Matador
Unit E2 Airfield Business Park,
Harrison Road, Market Harborough,
Leicestershire. LE16 7UL
Tel: 0116 2792299
Email: books@troubador.co.uk
Web: www.troubador.co.uk/matador
Twitter: @matadorbooks

ISBN 978 1803132 877

British Library Cataloguing in Publication Data.
A catalogue record for this book is available from the British Library.

Printed and bound in the UK by TJ Books LTD, Padstow, Cornwall
Typeset in 11pt Adobe Garamond Pro by Troubador Publishing Ltd, Leicester, UK

Matador is an imprint of Troubador Publishing Ltd

Dedicated to my husband, Michael Barker.

SKULL

THE BANQUETING HALL

ALCOVES

THE TRIANGLE

THE MINER'S CAVE

THE RIVER STYX

THE CURSING WELL

THE INNER TEMPLE

CHAPTER 1

Finding it awkward looking in her direction, I started to glance around the room. Her voice started to blend into the background, an echo now. *It's a nice space,* I thought; hanging plants from bookless bookcases, canvases of forests and sandy beaches, leaf-patterned cushions scattered on beige lounge chairs with beige rugs and curtains to match. Of course, it was all designed to make you feel comfortable and at ease, and to be fair, it worked. My mind started to wander again, back to what I was working on, what I was writing…

…Ivy stood on her balcony, overlooking the Inner Temple. Her people now called their kingdom a prison, and it was. But it was the only home she had ever known.

Twenty-eight years ago, her mother, the queen, had died in battle just days after giving birth to her. Ivy had become the youngest queen in her people's history, for kings did not exist. The entire kingdom was in disarray; the people had cherished her mother for she had been powerful, had led many battles and conquered many realms. Including this one.

Her father Arthur had lost much that day; their love for one another had been unmatched. The days of them fighting side by side were gone. Ivy had often seen her soldiers gazing at the many portraits of her beautiful mother, all commissioned by her father. He, however, would look up at them for hours.

With the kingdom in complete chaos after Ivy's birth, the enemies of the Inner Temple were able to assemble a thirteen-thousand strong army without her people noticing.

Nine days after the initial attack, over two thousand vampire soldiers and twelve witches had perished.

The demon army had also sealed shut the only gateway to the human world. Many demons had been left behind and became the vampires' only food source, buying them time to find a way out before they all starved.

"You'll get covered in ash if you stand out here for too long," her father said from behind her.

"I don't mind it Father, you know that," Ivy said absently.

After all these years the source of the ash was still unknown, and it continuously drifted from the sky so thickly that it protected her people from the harsh sun, the sole reason her mother had taken the kingdom.

"She's watching us again," Ivy said, unable to break her gaze from the ash fall.

"The female? Could she be a witch?" her father asked, sounding hopeful.

"No. Father? I know that I haven't seen one in the flesh or scented one, but I feel as though she could be human."

"Impossible."

"Maladaptive daydreaming."

"Huh, sorry," I said, embarrassed that I had spaced out in front of her, again.

"I said, maladaptive daydreaming, do you know what that means? Have you heard of that before?" Lucy asked.

It took me a few seconds to disengage from my thoughts. What was I thinking about? Ah yes, something that I had written the night before. I felt myself losing focus again. With all my strength, I concentrated on her face. She liked eye contact; it was something we'd been working on, but I still struggled, so I focused my gaze on her ever-changing glasses instead.

"Something about daydreaming," I said, as if it wasn't obvious.

I suppose you could call what I did daydreaming.

"Yes. What do you know about daydreaming? It's just that over the last few months that we've got to know each other you've told me that you researched a lot, trying to find information about why you could be feeling the way that you do."

"I'm sorry I spaced out. I'm just so tired. I was listening," I said, trying to be polite.

"Were you?" She smiled at me, patiently waiting for my reply.

She was still waiting; it was feeling awkward now. *Say something. Say something*, I hissed to myself.

"Er."

"You do that a lot, you know, space out, as you put it," Lucy said, with her patient smile still in place. "Do you want to tell me what you were thinking about just then?"

"I'm sorry, I lost concentration again, it wasn't important."

"It might be. Was it about your mum, have you heard from her lately?"

"No, and I really don't want to talk about her this week." Every session seemed to come back to her, my mother, and I was done talking about it. She had her life in France, and I had mine.

"Well," I started, wanting to change the subject but not go completely off track. "Apparently there was a study that found people daydreamt for about forty-seven per cent of the time, or you could call it being on autopilot, something like that."

"Really? How did you come across that study? Did you search for it?" she asked.

I liked the way Lucy fished for information. I thought I knew where she was going with this, and I let it play out. I'd been seeing my therapist for a few months now, and if I was honest, the sessions had helped, only by a little, but more than I'd expected, and Lucy was good at her job; she was genuine.

"Yeah, maybe I looked it up," I said, trying to remember the rest of the study.

Lucy tried to suppress her smirk, and this made me smile. I bet she'd have loved to say, "Zoe, you either looked it up or you didn't, which is it?" But she couldn't; this room and our time together was what she called a 'safe zone'. She wasn't pushy and I sometimes liked to use that to my advantage.

"Do you feel as though you're on autopilot for forty-seven per cent of the time? Or more perhaps?" she said, still fishing.

"I'm just tired," I said, yawning, proving my point.

"Okay. So, Zoe, we're coming to the end of our session, is there anything specific you wanted to discuss? Or anything that stood out to you?"

Hating this part of the session because I could never think of anything to say, I just repeated my weekly response. "Yeah, umm, no, not really. I'm still not sleeping, I either can't get to sleep or I wake up early, but that's mostly down to the neighbours now." I had always struggled to sleep but now it was almost impossible.

"I'm sorry to hear that, I really hope your situation changes soon, or that you can save enough money to move on. Is that still the plan?"

"Definitely, yes," I said with conviction, but even then, that could take years. My heart sank at the thought.

"Are you still writing?"

"Yeah, when I'm not too tired," I said with another yawn.

"And how are you getting on at work?"

"It's going really well." For now.

"Good. I remember when you first came to me, you had told me that you had done a lot of research, trying to understand why you were struggling at work and with life in general."

She bent down to grab a pen and pad from her bag. She said while writing something down, "Will you look up maladaptive daydreaming? You might find it interesting. We could discuss it next week."

"Is it to do with me spacing out? It is just a lack of sleep." Has to be.

"Could be lack of sleep. Just read a few articles and see what you think." She ripped the page from her pad and handed it to me.

"Okay, I'll check it out. See you next Thursday."

***

A car blasted its horn over and over. I jumped and swung around to see if it was directed at me, and sure enough I got the confirmation I was expecting. The middle finger over the steering wheel.

Once I got to work, I saw that my colleagues had already started cutting. I wasn't late, they just start as soon as they get in.

"You're late," Rob said to me, then winked at his client.

"No, I'm not, we don't open for another twenty minutes," I said, grinning at my boss. I quickly opened the staffroom door and chucked my stuff on a chair then rushed back out to get my station ready.

I started by oiling my clippers and sanitising my combs and scissors.

"Chop chop, Zoe, chop chop. I need a favour," he said, while he ran the clippers over the top of his client's head. "I've got a dentist appointment next Thursday for a root canal. Would you be able to cover me and take the Friday off?"

"Well …" What could I say?

"It's half-term next week, we'll be rammed," he said.

I had therapy with Lucy that morning. Something I wanted kept private. I quickly thought of an excuse. Rob was staring at me, making me feel awkward. He was waiting for my response. Time up.

"I can come in from eleven thirty, if that helps? But I'd like to keep my Friday if that's okay?" Please don't pry Rob.

"You're hardcore, Zoe, hardcore," he shouted for someone else's ears.

"Hey, Patch! Zoe's doing six days next week, she's a trooper."

Patch was laughing, his client smiling. Obviously, something went on before I arrived.

"I tried to take next week off, can't deal with the kids," Patch said.

"Think of the money," I told him.

"Yeah, think of the money. Patch, you're a work-shy slacker," Rob said.

Olivia, my other teammate, and I burst out laughing.

***

I flicked my gown a few times to free it from the last client's hair cuttings, then used my hairdryer like a leaf blower to clean my chair and station. I yawned into my hand before I faced the waiting area behind me, and felt relieved to see that we were coming to the end of our lunchtime rush.

"Okay. Who's next?" I called out.

An elderly gentleman acknowledged me with a nod, and struggled up from the green chesterfield. Another client sitting opposite stood abruptly, getting ready to help him up. I smiled to myself because I knew exactly what was about to happen next. Every client may be different, but I can predict the outcome of every situation under our barber shop roof.

Just as expected, my next client batted away at the good Samaritan's hands. He used the arm of the sofa as a crutch and heaved himself up. Once he was upright, he made his way to me.

"How are you?" I asked.

I put the brakes on my Belmont chair and watched while he struggled to get in, never offering help, because

I knew how extremely proud this type of client could be. Especially the ones who still wore a three-piece suit.

"I'm very well, how are you?" he said, pleased with himself.

"I'm good. So, it's been a while since your last haircut, hasn't it?"

"Is it that bad? It must be, because it was my wife that sent me here. She called me a scruff bag."

"Nah," I smiled. "Not at all, it's just a bit longer than usual. So, what are we doing? Back above the ears and above the collar?"

"Sounds about right, young lady, you know more about it than I do."

I flicked the gown one last time, then placed it around his neck. I picked up my scissors and comb and got to work.

"Are you going away this year?" I hated asking this question. Every time, every client. But it was the first question all us barbers used to get the conversation ball rolling. It was also a safe question. If the client was telling us about their trip away, then they weren't telling us about their opinions on politics and other topics that could lead to a debate.

"No, I'm not young lady, I'm too old for all that now. What about you?" I knew my client didn't really care whether I was going away or not, just as he knew I didn't care either.

"No, I'm too busy this year, it would be nice to get down to Bournemouth at some point." This was my bullshit response I gave every time.

"I was a coach driver," he said proudly. "Always driving people to the seaside, I was. You can't beat the British coast, young lady, I've seen it all."

Being new here at this barber shop, I had a lot of names to learn and forget. For whatever reason, nicknames were easier to remember, so I called this client, Coach Driver. I already heard some of my new colleagues refer to the clients by their nicknames. We had, Butcher, The One With Five Cats, White Socks, and my favourite yet, Shark Attack Terry. Shark Attack Terry lost one of his legs many years ago. He liked to tell people that a great white shark had bitten it off and then eaten it right in front of him while he was surfing in Australia. People said he was full of it, but apparently his story had never changed in all the years he'd been coming here. You just never know.

While my client told me about all the places he'd visited, his voice drifted into the background, along with the hum of clippers, hairdryers, the radio and the scent of Bay Rum.

I methodically used my comb to section off his hair, pull up cut, pull up cut, pull up cut. Then I felt my mind drifting back to what I had written the previous night. The story I was working on seemed to have taken on a life of its own. When I read through what I had written, I got weirded out by what I had ended up with. I certainly hadn't consciously written it. Well, some of it. I'd have to wait and see what David thought because, although my story wasn't going in the direction I wanted it to go in, I just couldn't bring myself to delete the bits that my sleep-deprived mind had written. It felt as though I could have been trying to tell myself something. Or maybe I was overthinking it.

"Young lady? That's a good job you've done there, my wife will be pleased," he shouted.

Bloody hell.

I looked down and saw that the haircut was complete. I appreciated my autopilot cutting skills, but I had truly spaced out this time. What was he saying? It most certainly wouldn't have been the first time I had flat out ignored a client.

He didn't seem upset, and I got a smile when I showed him the back. After I brushed off the loose hair and took off the gown, I walked over to the till that was behind my station. I gave him my biggest smile and asked if he was over sixty-five years old, knowing full well that he was. Our 'over sixty-fivers' got a five-pound discount, and well deserved too. They were a barber's favourite type of client.

"Young lady, you have made my day. I'm seventy-six next month," he said proudly.

"Oh really, you definitely don't look your age," I said honestly. "That's eleven then, please."

Coach Driver pulled out a ten and a five from his wallet and then squeezed it into my hand.

"You keep the change my dear."

"Thank you," I said in a small voice. I always got shy when taking such a large tip, and hoped that he didn't need the money more than I did.

"Young lady? If you don't mind me saying, you seem to have a lot going on in that head of yours. You need 'the me time' as my wife calls it." He smiled, then turned to walk out.

CHAPTER 2

Waking up a few minutes before my alarm surprised me. I might be wide awake now, but it would catch up with me later while I was working the busiest day of the week. Great.

About six months ago, my neighbour Wendy from below my flat, moved out to live with her fiancé, but instead of selling up, she rented her flat out. The letting agency for whatever reason rented that once beautiful flat to a pair of lowlife scumbags. My guess was that they were a couple.

They didn't work, so they slept all day and were awake all night. Drum and bass started around eleven, doors slamming open and shut as their loser mates joined the party, accompanied with shouting and singing in the communal hallway. I often heard my other neighbours screaming at them to "shut up", "keep it down" or "I've called the police", and yeah, the police came and went, but it all started again the following night.

The noise was something we all had to put up with, apart from the two bottom flats. Those flats were also rented out, and those tenants had the luxury of ending their contract early and moving on. We'd seen many removal vans come and go over the last few months.

So far, we hadn't received any help, not from Environmental Health, the council, maintenance or the letting agency. The truth was, no one really gave a shit because they didn't have to live with it.

But what really stung me was the treatment of their dog. I wasn't good on dog breeds, but to me it looked like a white boxer. I could be wrong. Ever since the scumbags moved in, not one of us had seen them walk that dog, so the poor thing had no choice but to use that flat as a toilet; this was evident due to the piss and dog shit smell that had taken over our communal hallway. The smell was so thick in the air that it clung to your clothing and hair in seconds. The stench had also crept into our homes.

According to animal welfare, house dogs were acceptable because house cats were legal. Unbelievable.

After a strong coffee I started my morning rituals. I gave up trying to use make-up to cover my dark circles; they'd spread above my eyelid and were heading down towards my cheeks. If they hadn't made me look so shattered, I'd have been happy to keep them, because they really brought out my green eyes. Silver lining, sort of.

Sandwiches made, backpack filled, Vans on, I was good to go.

As I reached for my front door I quickly sucked in a huge breath. This would protect my nose from that wretched smell, but once I was in the communal hallway, I could already feel it absorbing into my skin. I raced down one flight of stairs and knocked gently on the scums' door, knowing that they wouldn't be able to hear me. Their party had ended a couple of hours ago. I imagined them passed out somewhere; hopefully in their own puke.

It was the dog's attention I was knocking for, but hearing his little grunts and paw taps of excitement from behind their door brought me nothing but sorrow. I squeezed my hand through the letterbox as far as possible to stroke his face. He licked my hand and started to whine. My breath was starting to run out, so I quickly removed my hand and grabbed a treat out of my pocket. Once I posted it, I was off.

When I got to the front of our building, I saw the dog looking out the window at me while balancing on the back of a sofa. His only connection to the outside world.

"Who's a good boy? Bye, sweetheart."

I was failing him, but how else could I help?

I imagined taking him away and giving him a wonderful life, a life full of long walks, good food and no loud music. But too many hours away from home would make it impossible, even if I could get away with dognapping.

At that moment I was doing as many hours as possible. I told my boss Rob that I'd cover all sick and holiday taken by the others. He thought I was a 'star'. He wouldn't think that for long if the spacing out got worse again.

Six months ago, I was lucky to get two hours' sleep a night. You just can't function on that, so after I lost my job for being unreliable and a suspected drug user, I was desperate. I had to be quick about getting a new job or I'd lose my flat. Luckily for me, David, my stepdad, had heard about a girl leaving Rob's barbers to have a baby. I quickly raced down there and offered to do a trial day. For us that was how we conducted an interview. The boss saw how well you could cut, how good you were with clients and whether you'd make a good fit with the rest of the team. He didn't even ask for a reference, although I suspected he already knew that I got sacked; our town was small and word got around.

He was a good man for giving me a chance, and for that I would be eternally grateful. But in order to stay focused I had to go straight to sleep after work, then when the music started at eleven, I would get up and start writing, then around four in the morning go back to sleep. But in the last week or so I hadn't been able to sleep straight after work. I'd just been lying in bed wide awake, thinking about what I wanted to write.

I started my walk to work, thankful for the frosty morning. This woke me up faster than any amount of coffee could. I used this thirty-minute walk to go over what I had written the night before, while downstairs had the music blaring.

***

Clean-up started when the last client left. I yawned for the tenth time and apologised for the tenth time while Olivia told me about this amazing nail bar that she used while I cleaned the mirrors. Patch and Rob were asking each other what their weekend plans were while sweeping the last pile of hair in the bin. Almost done.

We walked out together and stood with Rob while he locked the door. Our barber shop was tucked down an alley next to the town car park. "This is why we're so busy, it's convenient for the clients, and we're the first barbers they see before heading into town," Rob had proudly told me when I first started, and he was right. This was the busiest I had ever been.

Olivia and Patch turned left towards the car park, and Rob and I turned right into the high street.

I saw Rob opening and closing his mouth, wanting to say something. This couldn't be good. My adrenalin spiked.

"Zoe? It might not be my place to say this but… you look really rough."

"What!" *How rude*, I thought. *Where did that come from?*

"Wait, wait. Er, that's not what I meant. I didn't mean to call you…" He laughed hard, then looked embarrassed. "Every time I tell my wife she looks tired she says 'rough, you mean' and for some reason that came out instead of tired. Sorry."

I laughed with him. It was the first time I'd seen him all flustered and I was enjoying it.

"Well, yeah, I am shattered," I admitted, still smiling.

"Look, I'm no expert and I'm in no rush to get home, so speak up or don't." Rob looked at me expectantly. Lucy was always saying that talking helps and getting things off your chest is healthy. I had a feeling that Rob would be understanding, maybe even a little sympathetic.

I tried to start from the beginning but all of a sudden everything just came out like projectile vomit, from the loud music and parties every night, to the poor dog's situation; police visits to either seize drugs, cars or whenever my neighbours call them; verbal abuse I received when I crossed them in the hallway; their friends banging on all our doors in the early hours of the morning. I told Rob about all the complaints my neighbours and I had made, only to be palmed off, and then I told him about how I lost my job.

"Bloody hell. I'll be honest, rumour has it you got sacked for being on something. You didn't look the type to me, and I would know," he said with a knowing look. Maybe he had someone in his life who had an addiction, or perhaps he did. I'll never know because I would never ask.

"You okay?" he asked.

I felt hot tears roll down my cheeks when I nodded yes. I looked down at the pavement, not knowing what to say.

"Okay. This is the plan, so stop your crying and listen," he said to me in a mock strict-parent tone. "You will go to the estate agent who let that flat to those wastrels and then tell them you want to sell your home—"

"But no one is going to buy a flat when the communal hallway has been trashed and reeks of dog poo and urine—"

"Exactly," he cut me off. "Think about it. The estate agents will be getting more commission from you than them, they will cut their losses and boot them out. Ta da."

"Ah, okay." I sniffed. "I didn't think of that. But even if I did want to sell, I don't have the money to move."

"They don't need to know that, and if they ask, tell them that a relative is going to lend you what you need. Are you going home to sleep now?" he asked while tapping the side of my arm. I smiled; this was his way of comforting me.

"Not yet. Do you know David who owns the second-hand bookshop? He used to be my mum's partner from years ago, but we stayed in touch, I'm just going in for a catch-up before heading back."

"Yeah, I know of him. Well, rest up as much as you can then, and know that you always have my ear and my incredibly good advice, free of charge of course," he said, still trying to cheer me up, and it was working, even if it wasn't that funny.

"Thanks, Rob, I really appreciate it. I'll see you Monday."

"Yeah, see you Monday."

My walk to David's shop felt good. I finally had a plan, a plan that might actually work.

***

As soon as I walked through the door I was greeted by Missy, David's little mixed terrier. She was an absolute sweetheart. I missed the times when Dave would go on holiday and I would take time off work to look after her, but thanks to my current situation I couldn't. It wouldn't have been fair to her. I went down to one knee and let her rub her face all over me.

"Good girl, Missy, good girl. Hey, David, how are you?" I said, standing back up to hug him.

For a slim man, David could give me one hell of a bear hug, and he was tall enough to kiss the top of my head.

"I'm always good, it's the others. How are you, poppet?" he said, sitting back behind his desk, wearing his usual checked shirt under a sleeveless jumper.

"I'm good, just tired."

"You're always tired. Hand it over then, what you've been working on," he said.

"David? I wrote something weird last night, something I can't remember writing. It's as if I'm typing in my sleep. Do you think that's strange, or not?" I looked for a frown or something to validate my concern.

"Maybe that's what's supposed to happen when you write, let your subconscious take over. In the end I don't suppose it really matters because it's still you, isn't it?" he said simply.

"Yeah, I guess." Maybe.

I pulled my laptop out of my bag and put it on his messy desk. I moved a pile of books so I could plug in the charger for my laptop. I scrolled down to where I left off and told him I'd be out the back with Missy. For some reason, I couldn't be in the same room as him when he read my stuff. It made me nervous.

When I got to the back of David's shop I started tidying up. There was no more shelf space so he just piled them up like skyscrapers. As I stepped over what looked like New York City, I knocked a few off the top. Picking the books up to find them a new home was impossible. I suggested once that he started selling his books online, but after the look I got, I made a mental note not to bring it up again.

David was proud of his bookshop, and called it an 'organised mess', and maybe he was right; I did always seem to find what I was looking for.

David called me over when he was done reading and my heart filled with dread. He could be brutally honest, which was good, but the truth could hurt. However, knowing that his criticism came with some good advice made it a little easier to swallow.

"So, I'll be honest with you, the vampire thing isn't for me, as you know. Show me the part that you can't remember writing," he said.

Oh great, he's more interested in that.

I picked up little Missy, placed her on my lap next to David, then faced the laptop to me. I scrolled up, then pointed.

... "She's watching us again," Ivy said, unable to break her gaze from the ash fall.

"The female? Could she be a witch?" her father asked, sounding hopeful.

"No. Father? I know that I haven't seen one in the flesh or scented one, but I feel as though she could be human."

"Impossible."

"Well, don't you think it's weird how I can't remember writing it? And how am I supposed to carry on if I don't know who 'she' is?" I asked.

"How about this, you just keep going as you are and maybe your subconscious will reveal it to you in time, and if it doesn't, then go back through it and revise it," he suggested.

I thought perhaps he was right; what harm could it do? Anyway, it wasn't like I expected to get anywhere with this story. It was just a hobby, something to pass the time, something to take my mind off things. Well, that's what I kept telling myself. *Yeah okay, I'll roll with it*, I thought.

"The vampire thing though, what's your spin?" he asked in a bored tone.

"I'm hoping to make them horrifying, to give them a serial killer vibe with no compassion, to be disconnected soulless creatures," I said, then sighed. Even to me that sounded pretty average.

"And what will they look like?"

"Like human—"

"No! Try again," he said, cutting me off.

"Listen! Like humans but with sharper features, skin like stone. A double row of teeth, pointed and serrated, like shark teeth but thinner. So instead of two little pinpricks it will look like the victim's neck has been mauled."

"And?"

"David. I can't completely change their appearance, because they will need to be able to blend in to the human world when they escape, so they can hunt," I pleaded.

He gave me an eye roll that said he was less than impressed. I, too, gave myself an eye roll. They did sound bland and boring.

"Will these vampires require a stake in the heart to die? What other weaknesses will they have?"

"No stakes, just decapitation. Possibly starvation. They will be able to tolerate the sun, but their eyes won't. For them to have perfect night vision their weakness will be to have no day vision," I said pridefully. He still didn't look impressed.

"And do these vampires bite others to turn them?"

"No, they can't turn humans. But they can breed, only with their own kind though."

"And where do these vampires live?" His tone told me he was still underwhelmed.

"Can you remember taking me to the Hellfire Caves when I was younger?" David nodded for me to carry on. "The caves had been man-made. Rumours of black magic and satanic rituals had taken place there, if you remember?"

"I do," he said, seeming pleased that I had remembered one of our day trips.

"The Inner Temple was inside that cave, and to enter, you had to cross the river Styx. In Greek mythology, the river Styx had been the boundary between the mortal world and underworld. My vampires are trapped in the Inner Temple."

"And how did they get trapped?" David asked, starting to sound interested.

Finally.

"Well, to cross the river, you had to pay the Ferryman. One coin for a one-way ticket, or two coins for a two-way ticket."

"What Ferryman?" he asked. I could tell from the glint in his eye that he was teasing me.

"David! It was you that told me the story. Anyway, when the Inner Temple's enemy attacked, they destroyed all the coins, hence why the vampires are trapped. But a lot of the demons had gotten left behind." *Come on, David.* I really wanted his approval.

"Interesting," was all he said at first. "I think it sounds great; I really do. I'm proud of you Zoe, and I can't wait to read the rest."

I flushed at the compliment, knowing that he wouldn't have said it if he didn't mean it.

"Thank you," I said, then started packing my laptop away.

David started to look awkward; he opened and closed his mouth a few times, just like Rob had done earlier today. Will he comment on my appearance too?

"Have you heard from your mum lately?"

Oh no, not that. He knew not to ask me this question and hadn't done in years, so why now?

"No, I haven't, and I can't remember the last time we spoke. Put it this way, the only birthday card I got this year was from you. Oh wait, I do remember the last time she rang, it was two days after my birthday and she was absolutely steaming. When I asked her how much she'd had to drink, she put the phone down on me," I snapped, immediately regretting my outburst.

"I'm sorry, poppet. It wasn't my intention to upset you. I shouldn't have mentioned it."

David looked hurt and it killed me. Out of all my 'dads' he was the only one who truly wanted to take on the stepfather role. He would take me fishing with him and tell me to watch out for mermaids; we would walk through the woods looking for witches; and we would search all day for the talking frogs that had been contaminated in the Witney rivers. We had fun.

But the one true gift that David had ever given me was a passion for books. He would always bring them home for me, then he'd quiz me about them when I was done. I'd loved him, and still did, but my mum had soon realised that owning a second-hand bookshop didn't bring in that much money, so she broke it off.

"It's not your fault. But I think that it's best if I just move on," I said, hoping that it would be the last time he brought it up.

"Okay, poppet. You get home safe then, and I'll see you Monday after work."

We stood up at the same time so that we could hug goodbye.

Trying to make light of the situation, I tugged at a lock of his greying hair that had grown over the top of his ear. "You need a haircut; you're looking a little unkempt."

"Well, if you know of any good barbers, let me know." He grinned. "And you look like death warmed up by the way, try and get some shut-eye."

***

The walk towards home filled me with dread. While rummaging through my bag for the keys, the scumbags walked out the front door. I was treated to a dirty look, which was fine; those I was used to. But then she tried to barge into my shoulder. I quickly sidestepped out of the way, and out of that confrontation. My neighbours were also regular spitters, so I flipped my hood up just in case. I knew they would love nothing more than a screaming match and that was why I would never give them one.

When my key was in the lock, I sucked in as much oxygen as possible, then raced to their door. I opened their letterbox. It took one quick tap of my finger to get the dog's attention. After stroking his face with my fingertips and letting him lick them, I reached in my pocket for another treat. My breath was running out.

The door behind me whipped open, making me jump. I lost my breath and ended up taking a huge gulp of that foul stench.

"Gary!" I snapped.

"I saw you through my spyhole. Come in then. Quickly!"

he said, trying to usher me through his door.

I snatched up my bag off the floor and rushed towards his door, almost forgetting the dog's treat. I turned back quickly to post it.

When I entered Gary's flat, I was greeted with a completely different smell sensation. There was an air freshener in every plug socket and car air fresheners hanging off every door handle. He had vanilla, winter spices, lavender and what could have been black cherry. Nothing could disguise that putrid odour from the other side of his door, not unless you overdid it like this.

I felt sorry for Gary; he had more to put up with than the rest of us. Sally and her husband and I were on the top floor. Gary, though, not only lived opposite the scumbags, but his bedroom wall was connected to theirs.

"I don't know how you can stand that smell," he said, screwing up his nose.

"I can't. I just hold my breath so that I can't taste it. Don't you feel sorry for the dog? If we can't bear it, imagine how the dog must feel."

"Of course, I do feel sorry for the dog. I had a dog growing up. Oh, how did you get on with animal welfare?"

"They said that you don't have to walk your dog by law. I said, 'can you just come over and see for yourselves?' They said that because I didn't have proof of abuse that they couldn't just turn up." I would have slammed the phone down if I'd have been on one instead of a mobile.

"How are we supposed to get proof if we never see the poor dog?" He frowned.

"Sally upstairs got the same response from them as well, and had asked that same question. My boss gave me a good idea earlier."

After I explained Rob's plan, Gary said it could work and

wanted me to let him know how I got on. I apologised for my constant yawning but when he started, we just started laughing and rolled our eyes. Laugh or cry, as they say.

***

BOOM BOOM BOOM.

I bolted upright in bed, which was now vibrating in time to the music downstairs. I searched for my phone in the dark. What was the time? It didn't matter. I put my PJs on and went into my kitchen. I made a coffee with two spoonfuls of granules, my usual these days. I got comfortable at my dining room table that was also in my kitchen, and switched on my laptop. I noticed that the music had gotten louder. Had it been that loud before?

I started to type…

…Ivy was playing chess with her father in his library. She told him that their only food source was running low, which meant they were running out of time to reopen the gateway.

"What do the witches say? Your queen is exposed," he informed her.

"The witches say what they have always said from the beginning."

Witches and vampires had formed an unbreakable alliance. It was believed that over a thousand years ago, a young vampire had saved an imprisoned witch from a demon soldier; she was to be his amusement. The vampire cut off the demon's head, then took her back to her coven. He then gifted them with the head, asking for nothing in return. The witches were sentimental like that.

"The gateway needs to be opened from the outside. If you take my queen, my bishop will take yours," Ivy pointed out.

"My knight is behind you. Can you send Umbra out to search for the one that's been watching us?" he absently suggested.

Umbra was a pure black cat that was also a phantom, a human phenomenon. She had died in the human realm, then had been resurrected from the afterlife and could now cross the boundaries at will, without gateways. She had belonged to numerous witches and vampires over the years and had now attached herself to Ivy. Umbra, however, had other gifts. Being able to project her visions and thoughts to Ivy had been very useful over the years.

"Take my queen then! But if my bishop takes your knight then your queen will take it. I have already sent her. She could also sense the presence watching us, and will be able to locate the source swiftly," she said, looking over the chessboard for her father's approval.

"Clever daughter, however, I would like to know something. If you can see that many moves ahead, then why..."

"Turn that bloody music off!" I heard, snapping me out of my trance, surprised that I could hear anything over the music. Then I heard thudding and doors banging. Something felt different this time; something was off. Were the police downstairs?

I quickly raced to my bedroom and dressed. I could hear Sally screaming that she had called the police from behind my door.

I opened my door and saw her and her husband both in dressing gowns. They were looking over the banister, both with shock etched onto their faces.

"Is that Gary shouting at them?" I asked, halfway down the stairs.

"Zoe, stay out of it," Sally shouted.

But I couldn't. Gary was my friend and he had been good to me. As I made it to the next flight down, I stopped dead in my tracks. My mind could not comprehend what my eyes were seeing. Time slowed.

The white dog had clamped his jaws onto Gary's elbow.

He was screaming, "Get off, get off."

The partygoers were chanting, "Get him, get him," and laughing hysterically. But all I saw was a frightened dog, with glazed-over eyes.

I ran over to the dog and wrapped both of my hands around his muzzle.

A muzzle covered in Gary's blood.

As gently as possible, I attempted to pry his jaws open. "Good boy, that's a good boy," I tried to say calmly, but my voice was shaky. I was shaking.

From behind I felt slaps and kicks rain down on my back.

"Get off my dog! Bitch!" the owner bellowed.

When I lost my balance and landed on my shoulder, the dog let go of Gary's elbow. I thought it was all over, until the dog whipped around and latched onto the scumbag owner's hand.

Even though I was sprawled on the floor with Gary, the irony of the dog's action wasn't lost on me. If I hadn't been in shock I might have smiled, even gloated.

Panic consumed me when the drunken partygoers started hitting and kicking the dog. No. I rushed to my feet and pushed this guy away who was about to stamp his foot down onto his back. I frantically called the dog to me. "Come boy, come on."

I got his attention. He let go of the mangled hand and headed in my direction. I ran up the stairs without looking back at Gary, but I could feel his eyes on me. Or perhaps he was keeping an eye on the dog that was now by my side.

"Zoe, he's dangerous. Don't take him into your flat," Sally said, while squeezing tightly to the wall, trying to create distance between us.

"It's not his fault," I said, before closing my door.

***

Once we were inside, the dog started to pace and whine. *What can I do, what do you need?* I mentally asked the dog. I knew what he needed. I slowly made my way to the kitchen, not wanting to startle him, and filled a huge pasta bowl with water. As soon as it touched the floor, the dog rushed over and started gulping it down. It was then that the true horror of the night showed its ugly self. Unable to believe what I was looking at; I took a seat.

Not only was the dog covered in blood from his nose down to his chest, but I saw every bone in his body and I saw every cigarette burn, too many to count. Some of the burns were fresh, which meant it must have happened as recently as tonight.

"Poor baby, poor boy." I was finally able to use my soppy doggy voice that I used for Missy.

When I kneeled before him, he came over to me, with a wagging tail, and hopeful eyes. All I could do was cry for him. I cried for him because I knew that at some point this frightened dog would be euthanised for biting someone.

He will be punished. For what? For being an abused animal who'd had enough.

***

A sharp knock made us both jump, and the dog started growling towards the door.

"Zoe? This is the police, we're coming in."

I was almost to the door when they opened it and passed through.

"We let ourselves in, in case you were in trouble."

He looked at the dog. "Everything seems fine, the animal control are five minutes away," the older police officer said. At the same time the other one went down to one knee to pet the dog.

"It wasn't his fault, he's been abused," I pleaded.

I heard Sally out in the hallway telling her husband that she could hear my voice and that I sounded fine.

"I'm Officer Blake and this is Officer Williams. We have a few questions for you, but that can wait until animal control gets here," he said curtly.

"What happened to you boy, what happened sweet boy?" Officer Williams said in his soft doggy voice. The dog responded with a small whine.

"He's going to be put down, isn't he?" I sobbed, with fat tears falling from my eyes.

Officer Williams stood up and looked at his colleague, and put his hand on my shoulder. "He might have a strong case if he's been abused, which he clearly has. He will receive medical treatment first, and both Officer Blake and I could vouch for him," he said in his Scottish accent, trying to reassure me.

It was then that I recognised Williams. He was a client from my barber shop. I had only seen him once and that was because Olivia had nudged for my attention and nodded her head towards his direction. His nickname was Hot Scot, but only used by her; Rob and Patch would rather die a thousand deaths before using it.

"You work at Rob's barbers, don't you? You're new there," he asked, smiling.

His devastating smile took me by surprise.

I examined him for the second time, the first time in the barber shop through the reflection of my mirror, and now, standing in my hallway. His hair was hidden under his police hat, but I knew that it was dark and thick, shorter on the back and sides, and longer on top, sweeping away from his face. I had watched Rob cut it. His eyes were a very pale brown, something that I hadn't noticed before, quite unique. If staring at his eyes counted as eye contact, then Lucy would be proud.

A muffled voice came through on Officer Blake's radio, just as I was about to answer Williams.

"Animal control are here now, so let's do this as calmly as possible, for the dog's sake," Officer Blake said.

I had assumed him to be a bit cold towards the situation. I was wrong. When he stepped just outside my door, I could hear him talking to animal control.

"The dog is harmless and needs medical assistance. He's all skin and bone, surprised he's still standing if I'm honest. Has the hallway been cleared from here to the front door?" he asked.

My heart lifted. Maybe he wouldn't be euthanised. He'd get rehomed, find happiness.

"Yes," animal control replied.

"Do you mind if I take that?" Blake reopened my door with a slip lead.

I watched Officer Blake go down to one knee.

"Walkies, walkies, come here then," he said while stroking the dog's face and chest, showing no concern for the blood that was still damp on his coat. "Walkies."

My heart broke because the poor dog probably didn't know what 'walkies' meant.

"What's his name?" Officer Blake asked, not taking his eyes from the dog.

"I don't know, I just call him a good boy." At the mention of my name for him, he started wagging his tail and sniffed me.

"Goodboy it is then. Come on then Goodboy, walkies," he said, then gently slipped the slip lead over his face.

Goodboy started to pull towards me when Officer Blake tried to lead him out the door.

"Can I walk down with him? He'll be frightened," I asked desperately.

"Of course, you can," Officer Williams said. He gave me another smile.

When we got outside, Goodboy started sniffing the air. Freedom. But not for long.

Blake slowly and gently picked him up and placed him in a cage that was in the back of the animal control van. He left the cage door open.

"Say your goodbyes, Zoe," Blake said, all businesslike.

I was stroking Goodboy while sitting in the boot of the van next to the cage. He lay down, whining softly as he started licking my hand.

"I'm so sorry I failed you, Goodboy. I'm so sorry. I tried getting you help, I did, but no one would come out." I was crying hysterically now, and I didn't care who saw. Goodboy looked up at me with those puppy-dog eyes, and I cried even harder. If anyone were to walk past right then, they'd think he was my dog.

"I'm so sorry you suffered like this, but these people are going to find you a new home, a home where people will love you and take you for long walks, okay?"

I was struggling to talk, so I leant down to kiss his head, then stood up to leave. As animal control closed the cage, I faced the police officers, surprised to see them both with tears in their eyes.

Officer Blake cleared his throat and Officer Williams looked down to the ground.

"Are you ready to give your statement, or shall we come back another time?" Blake asked.

Statement? Of course, they wanted a statement. While I thought if I could recall the last few hours with clarity, I saw a black cat watching us from across the street, out of place, and yet familiar. No. Impossible.

"I'll give you my statement now," I said, unable to break my gaze away from the cat.

***

Two hours later, both officers thanked me for my time. Officer Williams took my mobile number so that he could update me on Goodboy's progress.

One hour after they had left, Officer Williams phoned me to tell me that Goodboy had died on the way to the vets.

CHAPTER 3

After I put the phone down to Officer Williams, numbness spread throughout my body before guilt consumed me, almost bringing me to my knees.

I didn't understand it. He had wagged his tail when I stroked him. I lay back on my sofa, thinking of what I could have done differently. Should I have given him food? Could that have made a difference? Perhaps not. Williams had told me that when Goodboy's body arrived at the vet's, they had mentioned possible organ failure was responsible for his death. He had also told me that the vet would be taking photos of Goodboy's injuries for evidence, and making a note of how many cigarette burns riddled his emaciated form.

But what difference would it really make? Banned from keeping animals, goldfish not included. No justice.

While lying back on my sofa, I realised just how tired I was, and hungry. Well, my body was tired, but my mind was not. How long had I been awake? I should probably have slept, but my anger was preventing it. At least I thought I was angry until I heard the scumbags downstairs banging around. They had either just got back from the police station, or they had just woken up.

When I heard them laughing and joking around, my fury ignited. Rage boiled through my veins. I slammed open my door and headed towards theirs. Ignoring Officer Williams's advice to stay away from them, I pounded on their door.

As I was pounding, pent-up tension was released. I thought about all they had done, not just to Goodboy, to all of us. They caused us so much stress. I had lost a job; we had all lost sleep. We had all felt unwelcome in our own homes. Sally had stayed with her mothers-in-law on many occasions, just to have a break from the relentless noise. Gary stayed with his brother for days at a time. Enough. I'd had enough.

Now I was kicking their door, bringing my leg up so I could stamp down hard.

"Open your fucking door and face me," I screamed, still pounding and kicking. "You killed him! You killed him! And you laugh about it," I was screaming even louder.

"We'll call the police, bitch," they shouted from behind the door.

Typical bullies. As soon as they're confronted without their drunken friends, they cower.

"Call the police. But know this, now that he is gone, things are going to change around here, you fucking arseholes."

If they wanted to keep me up all night, I will start keeping them up all day.

"Zoe, Zoe, calm down," Gary said. I was so furious; I hadn't heard his door open. When I looked at him, my eyes diverted to his sling.

"Are you okay?" I asked, out of breath.

"I haven't heard you shout before… who did they kill? The dog?" He frowned.

"Their dog died on the way to the vets." Then I shouted over my shoulder, "Those waste-of-oxygen arseholes starved him and burnt him."

"The police are on their way, bitch," they said from behind their door again, probably looking at me and Gary through their spyhole.

"Come on, let's go for a walk before the police get here," Gary seemed unusually calm.

I gave the door one last kick, then followed him down the stairs.

As we walked aimlessly around the streets, he told me that Sally had been on the phone to the letting agency all morning.

"She said at first that the agency couldn't disclose personal information. But you know what Sally's like. She more than likely threatened this and that." He was grinning.

I nodded for him to carry on.

"Apparently, they haven't been paying rent, and the letting agents are in the middle of the eviction process. Great news, isn't it?"

I hadn't seen Gary this relaxed in ages. Since I moved into my flat three years ago, Gary and I had always had polite chit-chat: "how are you? Hi, bye". That changed when the scumbags moved in. Gary was constantly checking in with me, daily, asking if I was okay, and how I was holding up. His concern for me was sweet, but every time we spoke, he had notably aged. Deep frown lines and dark circles were now a permanent feature of his. But now, even though Gary had been bitten and ridiculed less than twelve hours ago, he almost seemed… young again.

"Yeah. You said in the middle, how much longer?" I could hardly believe what I was hearing, and I was still not entirely convinced. Could they claim squatters' rights, was that a thing?

"It takes two months, by law, and that was a month ago," he beamed.

"All that help we begged for, and we're finally getting it, because they stopped paying rent? Rent?" I felt my blood boiling again, so I changed the subject. "Your arm?"

"Oh. Er, thirteen stitches, because I'm unlucky like that I suppose," he joked. "And the slings to stop the stitches from ripping out, you know, because they're in an awkward place."

"You seem really happy, considering…"

Just as we turned into our street, a police car pulled up to our flats.

Gary put his sling-less arm around my shoulder. "Come on," he said. "Let's walk into town and get a coffee."

***

When I got back, I felt deflated, tired and weak, but I knew sleep wouldn't happen. I had too much on my mind.

I rang Rob and told him everything that had gone on over the weekend. My voice was slurred. I was about to put the phone down when I remembered why I rang in the first place, and asked if I could have tomorrow off.

"Of course," he said without question. He was really understanding and asked if I needed anything else. Very sweet of him, and I never forgot or took for granted those that had been good to me. Then I threw my phone on the sofa and wobbled to my table.

Still unable to get Goodboy out of my mind, I decided to add him to my story before I fell asleep. It would be my attempt to prolong his life, maybe to right a few wrongs. I could give him the life he should have had. My mind was already starting to shut down when I slumped down onto my chair, almost slipping off. I yawned then started typing...

...The queen's father, Arthur, paced from one side of the library to the other.

"There must be another way. We are running out of time," he snapped at the witches.

Both Hazel and Willow took this in their stride, both beautiful and lethal in their own right. With a quick flick of their wrists or a whispered chant, they'd have no problem snapping every bone in Arthur's body. But there was a lot at stake.

"The gateway cannot be opened without coins; the coins need to be brought in from the outside," Hazel replied in a bored tone. How many times had she said this, and in how many different ways?

"And what of you daughter? What did Umbra show you?" He softened his voice.

Ivy sat with her back to the trio with Umbra lying in her lap, both staring out the window at the ever-drifting ash. Without glancing back, she sighed. "Umbra has shown me much. The Watcher is young, perhaps my age." She paused, recalling what she had been shown.

At first, Ivy was distracted by the sights and sounds of the street. The lights were too bright. The Watcher's life was chaotic to say the least. Multiple humans shared her home, that was apparent. Cars with blue lights had been parked outside her home. The humans driving those cars were wearing identical clothing and armour. Ivy had quickly consulted her father's library of the world's knowledge before this meeting; she had discovered that they had been police officers, and she had felt foolish. How many times had she heard her people say 'police' in various conversations?

The police officers had gone into the tall building and then took humans out. The Watcher was the last to be taken out. However, the circumstances were different; she had left the building with two police officers and a skinny white dog.

"She seemed so ordinary, distressed but ordinary," she said distantly.

"Did she not vibrate with any power at all, my queen?" Hazel's hopeful question frustrated Ivy.

"I would have felt it, you know that. She's just a human," she said simply.

However, hope burnt through Ivy when the Watcher locked eyes on Umbra. Recognition. But she would keep this to herself. She would not fuel unnecessary hope.

Arthur was about to speak when a sharp knock on the door cut him off.

"My queen?" Varik said as he opened the door. "Dinner is served."

Varik, her most loyal soldier, swung the door wide and dragged a demon in by the ankles. The demon's neck had been snapped, paralysing it. But immortality was a beautiful thing, for the vampires' keen hearing could already hear the bones fusing back together.

The stench of these things was unbearable; their skin looked reddened and burnt; they wore little to no clothing, or whatever was left of their armour.

The only similarity they shared with vampires and witches was the dark-to-black hair, although theirs was now matted. Served them right, foolish demons.

Ivy finally turned to thank Varik when a white dog jumped over the demon's body.

"Goodboy," her father called.

"Hello Goodboy," Willow said in a sing-song voice.

The white dog bolted over to Arthur, jumped up and licked his face. Then he greeted Willow the same way, then ran to Hazel who was kneeling on the floor. Everyone's mood was instantly lifted, and Arthur's face lit up with pure joy.

Ivy looked around, confused. What was going on? she thought. Goodboy locked eyes with her, then pranced over. Umbra didn't react at all, she just reached out with her nose to say hello. When the white dog rested his chin on her lap, she ran her hand down his head. Comparing this dog to the dog that Umbra had shown her was interesting. The other had been covered in blood, tortured. This dog was well muscled; the shining white coat was unblemished; his whole demeanour was different. This one was confident... happy. Different, yet the same.

"My queen? May I take back the body once it has been drained?" Varik asked, then patted his thigh for Goodboy's attention. "Because my boy is hungry, isn't he?" he said, while stroking the dog's face with both hands.

"He doesn't look hungry to me. I believe he's the reason why we're low on food," Arthur joked.

Ivy shook her head. Since when had her father made jokes?

"And don't bring any more bodies into my library. The books will absorb the stench," he added.

"Forgive me, my lord. I'll take it to the witch's kitchen," Varik said seriously, then grinned at the witches. "And what about you two beautiful hags? Do you want an arm, a leg, or the organs?"

"Ew, Varik, how grotesque of you. I'll take the heart," Hazel demanded.

"No. You had the heart last time," Willow argued. "I want it."

Due to the constant ash drift, the witches were unable to grow food, and had no choice but to eat demon flesh. Not that they complained; they said that when the meat got cremated, it tasted like chicken. Although Ivy had suspected that this was a human saying.

"That will be all, Varik," Ivy said sharply, then turned her back to him.

Hurt flashed in Varik's eyes an instant before he bowed. "My queen," he said, then left with the dog and body.

"Ooh, lovers' tiff?" Hazel said, wanting a reaction.

"What's he done now?" Arthur rolled his eyes.

"Have you all gone mad? Have you?" Ivy stood abruptly, sending her chair flying. "You all act as if you have known that dog for years."

"You mean... Goodboy?" Willow seemed confused.

"Yes, Goodboy. That is what the Watcher called him. Can't you see? That dog was with her last night in the human world, and now he's here, with us."

"Daughter? Goodboy has always been with us, as cherished companion," he said, sounding confused.

"Father. We have been trapped here for twenty-eight years. How long do dogs live for? Or perhaps he had two coins for the Ferryman we didn't know about."

Arthur's handsome face turned to stone. He brought his hands to his nose to scent the dog. Both Hazel and Willow stood, stunned.

"If the Watcher had coins to send him here, that would explain it. But that doesn't explain why you all think Goodboy has always been with us, or why he knows us so well to greet us as he did." A thousand possibilities were rushing through her mind so fast, she struggled to pin one down.

"My queen? We must make contact with the Watcher."

CHAPTER 4

Asharp knock on my door woke me up with a fright. Fury flowed through my veins at being disturbed. I had fallen asleep at my table again. I didn't need to wonder who it was. She was calling out my name, over and over. I quickly glanced over what I had written. Watcher? What Watcher?

Bang bang bang.

"Zoe? Are you okay?" Sally shouted from behind my door.

Standing up sent a jolt of pain through my spine; my knees buckled in protest and I dropped to the floor. I was on my hands and knees, feeling bewildered and embarrassed in my own home. How long had I been sitting there? My stomach panged too. When was the last time I ate?

"Zoe? I know you're in there," she shouted again from behind my door.

"What!" I bellowed, shocked at myself. I found the strength to stand then stamped towards my door. I was unable to rein in my temper. When I opened the door, Sally was just stood there, motionless in her pink flannel dressing gown, perhaps startled. "Speak then", I wanted to shout.

"You spoke to Gary yesterday?" she finally said, in a quiet voice. "Did he tell you the good news?"

"Yes."

"Oh, er. Did I wake you? I noticed you didn't go to work today. I took the day off too," she said, still speaking quietly.

Guilt deflated my anger. Sally was a well-known gossip and nosy neighbour. But she was a good person, always kind to me, not a malicious bone in her body. It was clear to me that she just needed an ear. Lucy was always saying that it was good to talk, but I just didn't want to. Sally, just like Gary, had also changed in appearance over the last few months. Once a well-kept, beautiful woman, perhaps in her sixties, who wore a perfectly styled glossy bob, and was always immaculately dressed with diamond earrings, now looked tired, deflated.

"Yeah, you woke me," I slurred. "Are you okay?"

While she repeated everything Gary had told me yesterday, I thought of the happy life Goodboy had in my story. I gave him to a character of mine called Varik. I had felt sorry for him, knowing that he had feelings towards the queen, and that they would never be returned. Giving Goodboy to a callous vampire was risky and didn't feel right. Were my vampires cold-hearted just because they viewed humans as food? Was it not the same for humans to view a cow as food, but to then also keep and love a dog? I thought it worked.

"So, what do you think?" Sally repeated.

"I'm sorry, what?" I wobbled on my feet then used my door frame as a crutch.

"You're obviously very tired, I should let you go," she said, still standing there expectantly.

My phone rang from my kitchen. Yes! That almost never happened to me.

"I have to get that Sally," I said. But she just stood there, so I had no choice but to close the door in her face.

I almost didn't answer my phone when I saw who it was, but if I didn't get it over and done with, I wouldn't be able to put it behind me.

"Zoe, hello. It's Officer Williams. There was a disturbance complaint made against you yesterday from your neighbours. Didn't I tell you to avoid them?" he said sharply.

"Er," I said, caught off guard.

"Did you kick their door?" he asked, getting straight to the point.

"Yeah. But…" I said, giving up before I could think of an excuse.

"I'm going to ask you one more time. Did you kick their door?" he said, still using that sharp tone with me.

I had just admitted to it, so why… "No. I didn't," I said slowly.

"Okay, good. I can close this complaint. How are you today? Rob said you took the day off," he said with honest concern.

"When did you see Rob… oh no. You went to my work, didn't you? Were you wearing your uniform?" How embarrassing.

"I was. I'm sorry. I did explain to Rob that I just wanted to check in with you. He put two and two together, told me you had told him everything," he said quickly. All traces of tough officer were replaced with a nervous lad who'd been caught out.

"It's okay I suppose, I forgot you know Rob. Yeah, I took the day off, I knew I wouldn't be able to sleep," I slurred, then yawned. Now I was embarrassed for another reason.

"Are you okay? You sound strange."

I was just going to be honest with him. The last thing I wanted was for him to think I was a drug user, like my last employer. "I haven't slept since you left. Well… I may have had a few hours at my kitchen table." I yawned again.

"Zoe, it's the afternoon. Even I have rested since I last saw you."

"I know. I just can't sleep when I have stuff on my mind."

"Understandable. But you must avoid your neighbours—"

"The cat," I shouted. How could I have forgotten that cat?

"The cat. What cat?"

"The black cat. It was there when animal control took Goodboy. Did you see it?" I blurted.

Why was I asking him this? Oh no. Heat crept over my face.

"Er, no. No black cat. Zoe, I think you just need some rest. I wasn't on shift last night, but I heard there was another noise complaint made against your neighbours. My colleagues went over to put a stop to it. But I'm sure that also kept you up." His voice was gentle towards me now. I could have listened to him all day.

Wait, what did he say? Did he ask me a question? Something about a noise complaint. "Sorry, what did you say?"

"Your neighbours were playing loud music again. I'm sure that kept you awake."

No, it didn't keep me up because I was already up. I heard the police car come and go and I listened to the music go off then come back on again when they left. I just went back to writing. What else could I do?

"Hello…"

"Oh, sorry. Yeah, it did. Gary told me that they're getting evicted for not paying rent, so hopefully I won't have to put up with it for much longer," I said without enthusiasm. It just seemed to me too good to be true.

"That's good. Well, it's good for you, not the people they will be moving next door to next. Anyway, I'll let you go, and I'll see you soon."

"See me soon, why?"

He laughed. "Yeah. I'm due a haircut, or perhaps I'll see you sooner if you decide to have a good kick at their door again, who knows," he said, teasing me.

***

Staring at my phone while trying to process the conversation brought on a sudden headache. I wanted to think about Officer Williams, and wondered what his name was. But the thought of that cat won my full attention. Her name was Umbra; I had written about her before, when I was a child, back when David was with my mum. I had desperately wanted a cat, but my mum had said, "Never. No way." So, David and I would talk about what type of cat it would be if I could have one. He said it would have to be an invisible cat, so that my mum couldn't see. "What about the food?" I had asked, enjoying our game. "Mum will see it." David, always having an answer for everything, had said, "Perhaps she's a ghost cat. Ghosts don't need food, do they?"

I would just imagine what it would be like to have one, and would write about her in my diary.

Then the strangest thing happened when I was walking back from school. Out from the bush appeared this cat, the very same one from my mind. Green eyes like mine and a perfect unblemished black coat.

I remembered my heart sinking when she brushed up against my leg and I had felt her silky fur under my hand. Not quite the ghost cat I had imagined. But not all was lost, as she had followed me home.

David had got home from work first that day, and I was so excited to show him my cat. He couldn't speak at first, just stood there and tilted his head, which made me giggle. Finally, he'd said, "Zoe, where did you get that cat?"

"She just followed me home," I'd said.

Shaking his head, he'd bent down to look for a collar. "No tag. She might be missing so we'll look out for posters, okay?"

He'd told me not to let the cat in the house, just in case Mum saw. But I didn't listen. She would follow me to my room and curl up on my bed. I remembered my mum coming in to say goodnight; she'd looked straight at me and didn't even notice her. Maybe she was a ghost? She never ate food, and she'd just turn up without me opening any doors or windows. She would walk with me to school, yet nobody ever paid her attention. Even David had seemed puzzled by her. While stroking her, he'd absently said, "Umbra."

"What does that mean?" I'd asked.

"She's your shadow, following you everywhere you go, and when your mum comes into the room, she somehow blends into the shadows and disappears," he had said, not quite believing what he was saying. "Umbra means shadow, you should call her that." So, I did.

When David had to pack his bags and leave, I was left empty and shattered. No more walks through the woods, no more stories of witches, werewolves and mermaids, and no more ghost cats. It wasn't until I left school that I just walked into David's bookshop. Half of me expected him not to recognise me, but the look on his face was something that

I'd never forget. He didn't say a thing, just walked right up to me and gave me a tight hug.

From time to time I did think of Umbra and had purposely added her to my story, but to see her in the flesh again… it just wasn't possible, she would be, what… eighteen years old. Do cats live that long? I think they did these days. I would show David that chapter and see what he thought, see if he remembered her; he did name her, after all.

What else had I written? The Watcher; I supposed I was the Watcher. I clicked on the enter key to wake up my laptop, knowing I wouldn't have switched it off properly. It was dead. I looked for the charger and plugged it in. While I waited for it to charge, I made a coffee.

My heart rate spiked while I read everything I had written. I couldn't even remember doing it. All I knew before I started, was that I wanted Goodboy to be happy. How strange that my characters would talk about me or see what happened that night, and the coincidence of Umbra standing there. I had obviously been writing out what my subconscious had needed to release, or something like that. I didn't know.

The confusion I felt put more pressure on my existing headache. I needed to clear my head and take a break, but I couldn't. I reread it, over and over again. Ivy had said that if the Watcher had coins, then that would explain Goodboy's presence, but it didn't explain why all my other characters had always known him, and so well. But that was my plan, to give him a loving environment. What wasn't my plan was for Ivy to notice the addition of Goodboy to my story. I suppose Umbra had already shown her images of us together the night before, before I decided to include him. That must have been it. No, this was stupid, I was tired and not thinking straight. I gulped down my coffee and thought about making another.

Must make contact with the Watcher. What did that mean? That I needed to make contact with myself, that I was trying to tell myself something? No, that didn't sound right either.

Coins? Ivy said that I must have had coins to send Goodboy to the Inner Temple. Of course, that's what they would need to cross the gateway; I had decided that. How odd that a made-up character would come to that conclusion.

Unable to focus on the screen for much longer, I shuffled from my table to lie back on my sofa. I'd practise the breathing exercises that Lucy had suggested. Breathe in for five seconds, hold for five seconds, then release for five seconds. I repeated this a few times and felt all the tension leave my body, my muscles started to relax, my eyelids grew heavy. I even felt my mind starting to close down.

BOOM BOOM BOOM.

The music had started again. Early for them at four in the afternoon, and unfortunately too early for anyone to call the police. Noise complaints can only be made after eleven.

Unable to concentrate on my screen or sleep, I phoned David and asked if I could come down to his shop. Maybe he could help sort through my mess of a story and put my mind at ease.

***

Opening David's shop door felt like coming home. "Hey, David." Missy ran and jumped up at me before I could shut the door. When I saw him still sitting at his desk, making no attempt to get up, I panicked. "What's wrong?"

"Zoe, you look terrible, when did you last sleep?"

While I told him about my weekend, about what I had written and about seeing Umbra, I collapsed into the chair next to his and sank my head into my elbow. I could sleep just like this. But I wanted answers.

He was still reading what I had written. Perhaps rereading it.

"So, what do you think? Do you think I've gone mad?" I sighed. "I'm obviously the Watcher, but why would I write about myself like that?" When I looked up at David, I frowned; he looked as confused as I felt. He darted a look at me then looked out the window, making no attempt to answer. This wasn't like him, so I put my hand on his. "David?"

"I don't know where to start, it's a lot to take in, isn't it?" he finally said, rubbing his hands down his face.

"Just call me mad then, so that I can get this straight in my head, but you do remember Umbra, don't you?" If he would just tell me I was being stupid; I'd get over it. Or would I? Something niggled at the back of my mind, and it was trying to claw its way to the surface.

"I can't call you mad, although I will feel quite mad when I tell you what I know." He sighed heavily. "Before I go on, I want to know how far along you've gotten in your story. Are the vampires still trapped?"

"That's a random question. Yeah, they're still trapped but they think that if they make contact with me… I mean, if I make… wait. Do you know what, I'm exhausted. Sorry. I shouldn't have bothered you with this. It's closing time, I'll help you shut down," I said, standing up to lock the door. I stumbled over a few of his books, kicking them across the wooden floor.

"I've got it." He stopped me. "I'm just going to come out with it. Are you ready? The cat came after you started writing about her in your diary, correct? You used to write these little stories in it and if I'm honest I encouraged it. The cat scared me though, it wasn't real and yet I couldn't deny I could see it, sometimes touch it… and your mum, the way it would walk past her and she'd pay it no attention. I had asked her why she was no longer bothered by the cat, and she said, 'What cat, she's not having a cat." It was strange. At first, I thought you two were both trying to fool me, but you weren't that close." He paused for a few seconds and rubbed his hand down his face again.

I waited for him to continue.

"Then other things started to happen. Can you remember when we used to go fishing at Witney Lakes? You got a little bored once, so I told you to look out for mermaids. You were like a kid at Christmas." He smiled at this, and I did too. "We would make up stories about them and you would write them in your diary, you never left home without it. Anyway, after that there were many mermaid sightings, dog walkers, joggers and others fishing there would swear on their mother's grave at what they had seen, even my old friend Mike tried to convince me he saw one."

"I remember the rumours, it's probably what made you think of it in the first place," I said, trying to make sense of it, or perhaps trying to deny what I already suspected. I both wanted and didn't want to know the truth.

"No, Zoe. The rumours, or rather sightings, didn't start until after you wrote about it. That cat didn't turn up until you wrote about it. The vampires need to stay where they are, do you understand me?" he said, raising his voice at me.

All I could do was stare at him. Was this for real? It was. I mean, the thought of it had flickered through my mind when I was twelve, and yeah today, too. A niggle. But to have someone confirm my irrational thoughts was… well, I felt conflicted.

"And the witches in the woods, where did they go?" I asked, already knowing the answer.

"I suggested to you that they'd be better off in America, New Orleans. I convinced you they'd be happier and be able to blend in more efficiently, and so you wrote a story about how they had travelled there. We never saw them again after that," he said, still rubbing his hands down his face. That's when I noticed that they were shaking.

The shop had been closed for an hour now and the sun had gone down. Neither of us made a move to switch on a light. "So, where do we go from here?" I asked.

"It could all be a coincidence, I suppose. It's not, but it could be," he said, more to himself than to me.

"Yeah," I mumbled. "If it's what we say it is then what does that make me? I mean, what is someone like me called?"

"Well… I don't know, poppet. I don't think there is a name for it."

"I've written many stories before, so why now?"

"Your stories have been about regular people so far, boy-meets-girl type of stories. You once wrote a story about a colony of bats and their plight. Who's to say that those characters aren't walking and flying about?" He shook his head. "This is the first time you've gone supernatural… since you were a kid, anyway."

"If I wrote a story about us winning the lottery, why wouldn't it come true?" I knew in my heart that it didn't work like that; but why not?

"Creating characters is very different. You gave your characters likes, dislikes, personalities, lives. I don't know, you've given them a voice, hope, a purpose… a survival instinct."

***

After locking up we walked slowly to his car. Everything seemed different now, and if I wasn't exhausted before, I was now. Tripping over my feet and yawning was a blessing that broke up my stacked thoughts, bringing me back to my surroundings.

"Zoe? Hello, did you hear me?"

"Sorry, what?"

"Stay at mine tonight, so that you can sleep through the night. It would make me feel better if you did." This wasn't the first time he'd offered me his sofa.

"Nah, I appreciate the offer, but you know I don't like to be a burden, and you know how I feel about being run from my own home. I worked my arse off to get that flat," I slurred.

"What was that? I can barely hear you. Actually, do you know what, I'm not taking no for an answer. You look ill, you can't even walk in a straight line. You need sleep. We will drive to yours, pack a bag and you'll stay at mine."

"Okay, okay. Thank you."

***

David's bungalow was pretty much a duplicate of his shop; books were piled all over the place, with chessboards and pieces placed on top of those piles. I couldn't remember the last time we played chess with matching pieces. The only bit of green carpet I could see was under the glass coffee table. Most people would find his chaotic hoarding stressful and frustrating, yet it comforted me. I always felt at home here.

"I'll make us dinner. I won't ask when you last ate because I could hear your stomach rumbling in the car. You want beans on toast?" he asked.

"Yes please," I said, as I watched Missy navigate through the maze of books until she fell from sight. While David had waited in the car for me to grab what I needed for work, I knocked on Gary's door to tell him that I wouldn't be home. Turned out he had the same idea. The music was still on. The neighbours below and a few partygoers were in the communal hallway, in between my flat and his, drinking and stubbing out a cigarette next to the no smoking sign. "Excuse me," I said, hating that I had to be polite to these arseholes, but they just stood there, looking forward to a potential conflict. Pushing past them earned me a few rounds of "bitch" and "fucking bitch". As I walked past, I felt spit spray over my hair and hood. Crushed that this was my home life, I let my tears fall.

"Did you remember your laptop?" he asked, snapping me out of my trance.

"Yeah, I got it. I would say hope you like it, but I have a feeling you're going to put a stop to my story."

"Just need to keep them trapped, that's all."

"David, I wanted to keep things as accurate as possible, and the Ferryman charged Obol coins. You can only get them from auction sites now, so…" An idea came to me. Could it work? If everything David had said and I had thought was true, could it work?

"So? What are you saying, that your story wouldn't have worked out anyway?" He seemed pleased by this.

"That's right, I could have changed the coins, you know, used pennies instead, but that would have been too easy. I didn't think that far ahead." But now I was.

***

Even though we ate at the table, I still managed to spill beans all down my lap. Lifting my knife and fork felt like lifting weights.

"Ready for bed? I'll get you a duvet. Missy will wake you up early for a pee, but if you go down now you should get your eight hours. That alright, poppet?" he said, still looking worried for me.

"Thanks for letting me stay," I slurred.

He bent down to kiss my head then picked up a book from one of his piles on the way to his room. When his door closed, I grabbed my laptop from my bag. Right, I needed to word this perfectly. I'd need to get what I wanted across clearly. I typed…

> …The Watcher will place two Obol coins in Umbra's mouth in exchange for a service. She will cross the gateway to the Inner Temple. Ivy would take the coins for the Ferryman…

But how would Ivy get from the Hellfire Caves to Witney? My eyes were heavy and my head kept rolling back, but I needed to complete this; enough was enough. Think. Think! I furiously pounded at the keyboard…

> …The Hellfire Caves were filled with many gateways; the vampires used them to travel across the world. Once Ivy crossed the boundary, she would use another gateway, this one being a short distance from the Watcher's home. It was called the Minster Lovell Hall, now in ruins, protected by the Mistletoe Bride.
>
> "On her wedding day, the young couple had decided to play a game of hide and seek. She chose a chest in the attic. When the lid closed, it locked from the outside, trapping her inside. The wedding guests had eventually given up the search; however, years

later when the attic was cleared, they had found her skeleton curled up in the chest, still wrapped in the white gown," Arthur said.

"I know the story, Father," Ivy said, trying to hide her apprehension. To venture into the human world should evoke some other emotion than fear, but the unknown and her duty to free her people weighed heavily. She looked out over her balcony, seeking solace in the falling ash.

"You will need to pay the Mistletoe Bride a sixpence to cross the boundary. You will slip it into her left shoe, something her father had forgotten to do on the day, hence her bad luck," he said, cupping Ivy's hand and placing the coin in her palm. All gatekeepers demanded payment; always coins.

"And what of her enemies? The humans that she wants me to destroy?" Ivy now knew that they were the ones responsible for Goodboy's death. If the Watcher is a witch, then perhaps the dog was her familiar? *But why not kill the humans herself?* she wondered.

"Nothing in life is freely given. The Watcher wants payment. You will need to feed regardless, to me, this is a small price to pay. After that you will acquire more coins," he said...

Unable to focus on what I had just written, I mentally pushed myself to do one last thing before I passed out. Using my phone, I searched for what I needed. Sixty-five pounds each! Oh, but it will be worth it. If everything David and I had uncovered was true, then soon my nightmare would be over, and after what they did to Goodboy, let's just say my conscience would be clear.

Est. delivery Mon 6th. I clicked pay now.

CHAPTER 5

"Wake up! Poppet? Wake up."

"I'm up," I snapped. "You made me jump," I said as he shook my shoulder. "Stop."

"The kettle didn't wake you; the radio didn't wake you, Missy jumping all over you didn't wake you. Tell me, poppet, what does it feel like to sleep like the dead?" he chuckled.

Trying to find my bearings, I let my feet slump to the floor. I felt something hard under my foot. It was my laptop, still open and probably still on. I smiled to myself, remembering what I had done last night, then alarm bells went off at the thought of David noticing my laptop not being where I had left it. He would be angry at me for not going straight to sleep; even angrier if he found out what I had done.

"Beans on toast again?" he shrugged. "That's all I got."

"Yeah, that's good, thanks," I said, standing up, stretching.

"I'll drive you to work and then I want you to walk to mine when you're finished. I want you back here for one more night, okay?" he said gently.

I had slept well, or more like passed out, and although I was still extremely shattered, I felt better than I had in a long time. Sleep was only partly to do with it.

"Yeah, okay." I yawned loudly.

"Not arguing this time? Oh, one more thing before I put the beans on. If you didn't think that I noticed your laptop by the sofa this morning, you're wrong. If you're sitting there wondering 'shit, did he read it?', you'd be right."

Heat crept over my body. I wasn't ashamed at what I had done, just at being caught out and disappointing David. Unable to look in his direction, I said, "Now that we've both slept on it, don't you think it's ridiculous? Anyway, I can't remember what I had written. I was half asleep." Poor comeback and not entirely true.

"You know what you're doing. You made a deal with them but, towards the end, when you were clearly not in control of what you were writing, your characters were conspiring to get more coins. Did you catch that bit, or would you like to take the time now to read it?"

I vaguely remembered that part, I had to admit. But it was okay; Ivy wouldn't be able to get more coins. She was born into a world with no technology and wouldn't be able to buy Obol coins; plus, she would be so bewildered, she'd have no choice but to retreat with the remaining coin. Or would she? The pang in my heart confirmed my guilt, but not for the deal I had made. It was for Ivy. I just wanted my life back.

Turning into his kitchen, he said, "Do you know how many people across the world would love the opportunity to off their neighbours and get away with it? Millions. But could they really go through with it, live with it?" Raising his voice from the kitchen, he added, "Could you live with it?"

"Yes," I said coldly, hoping that it was out of earshot.

"For what they've done to you? It's wrong, but do they deserve to die for it? There are far worse people out there. Do the right thing. Do not order those coins, or just delete the story and start again. Give them a new world, create one that doesn't involve our reality."

***

On the drive to work, David tried to give me the 'difference between right or wrong' speech. I just sat there thinking about a quiet life, the one that I had before, but took for granted. Never again would I take it for granted. My only concern now was whether Umbra would show; after all, this could still be a wild speculation. A tightening in my chest told me that I was desperate for this to not be the case.

From the car park to work, I kept my eyes peeled for that cat. Nothing. My heart sank. When I entered the barbers, I said my 'hellos and good mornings' to everyone and went straight to my station to oil my clippers and scissors for the day. Rob and Patch were arguing about whether Patch was under the thumb or not in his new relationship, and Olivia was on the landline telling a client what time we closed for the day.

"Hey, Zoe?" she said before putting the phone down. "So… that Hot Scot came in yesterday, I didn't know he was a police officer. So, what happened?" Olivia asked, looking both concerned and greedy for gossip. "Rob said you had a hard time over the weekend."

"Yeah, I did, I was a bit shocked and embarrassed when I realised, he was a client of ours." I blushed. I'd have to hide in the back when he came in next.

"Don't worry about that," she said casually. "Tell me what he was like. He normally just waits for Rob for a cut, so I haven't met him properly."

I stuttered at first, not knowing how to answer that question. He was lovely, I wanted to say, then Rob opened the blinds and door, and four clients walked through. I felt relieved having got out of that one. Anyway, best not to think about him. Olivia abruptly turned and called a client over to her station and I called over the second one to mine.

The day went by in a blur. All I could think about was coins, cats, a quiet life, having more time to write, Goodboy and Varik, Ivy and her father, the Ferryman and the Mistletoe Bride. The Mistletoe Bride was a great addition to my story, and provided a convenient shortcut. I smiled to myself, then thought of David. Was he right, could I really go through with it? I felt that I could, but what about after? He did offer me his sofa until the neighbours left; that was if they left. I wasn't entirely convinced it could be that simple. All the possibilities whipped through my head like a tornado with no intention of slowing.

"Zoe! What are you doing?" Rob shouted from his station.

I jumped and snapped my head towards Rob. "What happened?" I looked around the shop, then down at the top of my elderly client's head. I saw nothing out of the ordinary.

"He," Rob said, pointing at my client with a nod, "asked for a scissor cut. You have just clippered the back and sides off." He looked at me accusingly.

Oh shit.

I looked down again at my client. I felt disorientated, unable to focus. What had I done? Why?

"I'm not happy, Rob, I'm not. I could tell she wasn't listening, is she even qualified?" He gripped the arm rests, looking absolutely furious with me, and rightly so.

"She is qualified. I can only apologise and correct your haircut," Rob said calmly, trying to placate him.

"Correct it how? There's nothing left to correct," the client said, raising his voice even higher. "I look like a thug."

Every person in the shop was now staring at us and I had never felt so embarrassed in my life. There was nothing I could do to put this right.

"Zoe, wait in the staffroom," Rob said, waving me away.

I heard my heart thumping in my chest after I closed the door. What had I done? I couldn't even remember him sitting in my chair, or asking him what he wanted. Oh no, that must have been it. It wasn't like this hadn't happened before. It had; it was how I'd lost my last job. I'd just grabbed my clippers and gone for it. I couldn't lose this job; they were one of the best teams I had ever worked with. Plus, this really was my last chance. With the bad reputation I had got for myself, there were no other barbers within a twenty-mile radius that would take me on. Hot tears streamed down my cheeks.

I heard Rob from behind the door relentlessly apologising to my client, and the client saying that he would never return. "I'm not coming back here, not after she butchered me." Then I heard the front door slam as the client left and Rob apologising to everyone in the shop.

After a few minutes the handle to the staffroom door dipped down, then back up. Rob must have been contemplating what to say to me. Had I already lost my job?

The door opened slowly. "Are you going to tell me what happened?" he asked, sounding surprisingly calm.

"I obviously didn't hear—"

"You didn't hear because you weren't listening. You have ignored your clients all day. The client before that one, Heart Attack Jack, was trying to tell you about his latest stint in hospital, but you just blatantly ignored him. I know it's boring bullshit half the time but that's a part of our job, to listen. I had to apologise to him on the way out and tell him you're going through a hard time."

"I know, I'm sorry. My customer service is good—"

"Not today, it isn't," he shouted, making me jump.

He breathed in and out slowly, trying to calm himself. I held my breath.

"I want you to take the rest of the day off. You look like you haven't slept in days, and you should have after having yesterday off." His voice lowered. "I took a chance with you, Zoe. You will not let me down; do you hear me?"

"I have slept. I stayed at David's house last night. Please let me stay. I'll do better, I'm focused now," I pleaded.

"I can't risk it, Zoe. This town is small, word gets around fast, and you know that."

"You're not sacking me?"

"Not yet, but I have Olivia and Patch to think about too. When the shop starts losing clients, we all lose money. Patch is saving up to buy a house and Olivia is saving up to get married. As their boss, I feel that they are my responsibility, as are you, under my roof. Go home and rest."

I nodded and silently got my things together before I did the walk of shame through the shop. Olivia gave me a knowing smile and Patch, trying to diffuse the unpleasant atmosphere, cheerily sang, "See you tomorrow, Zoe."

***

Unable to see David right now, I stormed back to my flat, furious at myself and furious with my situation. As I turned the corner, I saw Gary standing outside our building. He saw me, waved me over then turned his back to me to continue talking to… oh, not again.

The police were here again. As I headed closer towards Gary, I saw two police cars and a fire engine parked around the corner. Maybe the scumbags downstairs fell asleep with a cigarette still in hand. Maybe they burnt to death. I smiled to myself. I didn't see an ambulance, so no casualties. Knowing my luck though, it will just be theirs and my flat above that would have gone up in flames.

"Zoe, you weren't home last night, were you?" Gary asked, before the police officer could. Then I recognised who it was.

"Officer Blake," I said. "No, I wasn't home. What happened?"

"A fire in the communal hallway—"

"Let me guess." I smiled sarcastically. "Was it close to the front door, our only exit in case of a fire? Of course, it was."

I turned to Gary. "Where is Sally and her husband?" I panicked, instantly regretting the way I had spoken to her yesterday.

"An ambulance took them to the hospital. They inhaled smoke and are being checked over." Gary sounded both worried and angry.

I then turned to Blake. "I take it that no arrests have been made. Another guess of mine is that they fled the scene, leaving the rest of us to burn to death, because they had no way of knowing that Gary and I weren't home. I'm right, aren't I?"

"We're searching for them as we speak."

"And you'll find them, probably in the next few hours, you'll charge them with arson and whatever else, and then what? They will come back here and it will all start again," I said aggressively. Not my usual style, especially when Blake was only trying to help. I shook my head. "I'm sorry."

Blake's eyes softened before he spoke, "That's okay. We see this all the time. I understand that they are being evicted. From now until then I will have a car out front."

"How did you know I wasn't in?" Gary asked me.

"I knocked on your door to tell you I was staying at David's." And then I got spat on, so I decided to order two Obol coins for a murderous character from my story to kill our problem.

"Hi, Zoe. Sorry we have to meet again like this."

I turned to see Officer Williams walking towards us. I quickly ran my hand through my hair. Both Blake and Gary nodded to him in acknowledgement then walked back through the door, probably to look at the damage I hadn't the heart to see yet.

"I know you weren't home last night, but did you see anything worth mentioning?" he asked.

"Friends of theirs were hanging around in the communal hallway and spat at me as I walked past. Not that that helps the case in any way," I said, deflated. I really wished he wasn't here again, to see me like this, and my home life. How embarrassing.

"Ah, disgusting. Sorry to hear that. I have to say we were all very worried when we arrived, we didn't know who was in and who wasn't. Gary has called for a locksmith because you will both need new locks."

"Anything else?" I didn't even know if I had the money to pay. Especially after paying a hundred and thirty pounds for two fucking coins; for something that might not even work.

"Who is David? Is he your boyfriend?" he asked, looking shy all of a sudden.

This was none of his business, and he knew it. But why would he ask? I mean, it wasn't like he could have been interested in me, could he? I flushed at my own stupidity.

"He's my da… umm, stepdad, or at least he was," I said quickly.

He smiled at this.

"Will you be staying there again tonight? I have a feeling that your neighbours won't be back anytime soon, not when they see a police car out front waiting for them." He smirked.

"I don't know, if I'm honest. I feel a little overwhelmed right now. I had a terrible day at work, hence why I'm back early, and now I obviously need to pay for a locksmith, and that's all before I've even seen the damage. Does it look really bad in there?" I sighed. My eyes began to water.

He stepped closer towards me so that he could put his hand on my shoulder. "The walls and carpet are burnt, and the hallway has been vandalised. Maybe you should stay with David again tonight, so that you're not on your own."

He lightly squeezed my shoulder then ran his hand up and down my arm. My tears fell and I stepped closer to him. His hand on my arm felt good but I wanted more. As if reading my mind, he looked about awkwardly, then wrapped his arms around me. I assumed he was making sure no one was around to see; my guess was that this was frowned upon. Feeling his hands run up and down my back comforted me. The sound of me sniffing back my tears made him squeeze me tighter. When we heard Blake and Gary coming out of the building, he abruptly let me go and stepped back.

"Hey, Zoe," Gary said. "Are you alright? The locksmith will be here soon."

As if that would make everything okay. No, I shouldn't have been ungrateful. I might have had shitty neighbours, but I also had great ones too.

"Thanks, Gary. I'm going to stay at David's again. While I'm up packing a bag, does anyone want a tea or coffee?" I asked, hoping that they would all say no.

"Yeah, I'll have one, thank you," Blake said.

Oh great.

"I'll come up with you," Williams offered. A knowing look passed between him and Blake. Bloody hell, what else had gone on here?

Seeing the damage done to our homes broke my heart. It wasn't just the burnt carpet and black walls that were noticeable; there were cigarette butts littered everywhere, as well as smashed bottles and cans. It also reeked of urine. Oh, for fuck's sake, was that a used condom?

Feeling embarrassed, I attempted to explain my current living conditions. "It was never like this, you know, it was always clean and tidy. We were all very house-proud."

"I know it was. Look, Zoe, before we reach your floor, there's something you should know. The upstairs landing has been vandalised, but it can be repainted," he said, trying to lessen the blow before I saw it.

Dread consumed me. I stood still only for a moment to prepare myself, then slowly walked the last flight of stairs. 'Bitch' and 'slut' had been spray-painted in black all over my door, and Sally's too. A dark, wet stain at the bottom of my door told me that someone had pissed against it. I said nothing. What was the point? It wouldn't change anything. I reached into my bag for my keys, forgetting that I no longer needed them, then pushed open my door.

"Are you okay?"

I nodded.

"I'm sorry. I do think that this is also the responsibility of the letting agency to pay for the damage, if that helps in any way," he said, trying to make me feel better.

"They'll demand proof, I suspect. They'll do anything to get out of paying."

"Well, someone needs to pay for this."

"Yes, they do," I said, and they will.

Williams stood next to my kitchen window. The view was impressive, and I knew he'd be impressed with it too. It looked out onto a shallow river, surrounded by willow trees and tall reeds. The road in front of our flats was the bridge that went over it. I had often stared out the window, watching the ducks go about their daily routine, while drinking my coffee. It was a view that you could never take for granted. I put the kettle on and got the coffee out.

"What was it that your colleague wanted? Er, Officer Willi—"

"Just call me Bowen," he said, still looking out the window. "He always has coffee with no sugar."

Bowen. What a lovely name. It suited him.

He tapped at my window. "Hey, is that the cat you were talking about yesterday?"

Almost dropping the coffee, I darted to the window to see. Without giving Bowen a chance to move back, I stood behind him so that I could look over his shoulder. Yes! It was her, looking up, watching intently. Soon this would all be over, soon I would get my life back. I just hoped that she came back when the coins arrived.

"Creepy-looking cat. It's not yours, is it?"

"No, she's not." That was interesting, I thought. Bowen could see her too, as well as David.

CHAPTER 6

After a few days at David's, I was back at mine. I almost threw my parcel on the floor while I struggled to unwrap the packaging. Scissors. Had I got my scissors out of my draw in the first place, I would have opened it already. I cut open the packaging and found what I was looking for tucked in-between the bubble wrap. I was amazed at how small the coins were in my palm. I felt in control, empowered. I rubbed my fingertips over them while standing at my kitchen window.

The last few days had gone by in a slow blur. Seeing Umbra every day, watching me from outside work, or walking to David's shop, kept my spirits high. She was waiting for me. So close. But she wasn't there now.

I hadn't written a thing since being sent home, just replayed in my mind over and over what I wanted to write next, and thinking about how to not get monkey-pawed in the process. This couldn't possibly go wrong, could it? The thought of it not working at all was pushed to the back of my mind.

David had demanded that I stay with him all week, and I was happy to. He said that I could have been burnt to death if I were home and if the fire had gotten out of control. He added that it was only a matter of time before something else happened. He was also pleased to see me without my laptop, assuming I'd taken his advice.

But I needed to come home. There was something I wanted to finish.

It was late when I heard someone messing around outside my door. I checked to see if the police car was still parked out front, then looked through my spyhole. I put the coins in my jeans pocket then opened the door.

"Hi Sally."

She was repainting the hallway in her red and black tartan pyjamas. She looked tired, depressed; her hair scraped back into a short, greasy ponytail.

"Hi Zoe, how have you been?" She didn't look up.

She was rollering white paint over the black, but I could already see it bleeding through. It will take more than a few coats to cover it.

"Yeah, I've been okay. Sally? There's no point in doing all this until they move out, plus the letting agency should be doing it."

"True, but the agency said we had to prove that it was the two shits that did the damage and not their friends," she sighed. "Apparently, they weren't in. Have you been to work?"

"Yeah, I have, apart from that day I got sent home. I'm on my last chance now."

"My boss has told me to take an early retirement," she said with a humourless laugh. "I'm thinking about it, I'll be honest, just so I can sleep. But I don't want to spend my retirement calling the police every other night or repainting the hallway every week or spending the day at the hospital because some idiot thought it would be entertaining to start a fire."

She threw the roller back into the tray, splashing paint all over the carpet.

"Oh, now look what I've done."

"It's okay. We'll need a new carpet anyway, but we'll get it after they've gone."

She didn't reply.

Not knowing what else to say, I asked, "How's Gary been?"

"He came back Friday, I believe. But when the music started, he knocked on my door to tell me he was going back to his brother's. He's been asking about you, pleased that you're staying away."

"We shouldn't be forced out of our own homes like this." I sighed.

"No, we shouldn't, but we have tried everything, haven't we?"

"We have. I'll give you some money towards the paint."

"No, you won't. This is leftover paint from when hubby painted the living room," she said, her eyes watering.

"What's wrong?" I asked. Stupid question. We were all at the end of our tether.

"Hubby's gone, wants a divorce. Told me he couldn't live like this anymore."

I leant against my closed door, unable to think of what to say. What do you say? How could I make this situation better? David had asked if my neighbours below deserved to die for what they had done. Probably not; there were far worse crimes than the ones that they had committed. In fact, their behaviour was barely considered a crime these days. But why should decent people suffer just so they can have a laugh? How many times had they laughed when they put a cigarette butt out on Goodboy, or took joy when he whined and pleaded for food? If they were to be moved on, they would only ruin some other people's lives. I had already made up my mind when I got sent home from work, but now I had the confirmation that I'd be doing the right thing. I'd be doing the world a small favour.

"I have a spare roller, I'll help. I got a radio too and I'll make us both a coffee."

Painting the hallway was pointless, but Sally obviously needed to keep her mind busy, and she was perhaps in need of some silent company. Something I was good at.

"You don't mind?" Her small smile trembled. She held out her arms for me to walk into them. We hugged tightly, then she sobbed.

***

The first night in my home felt strange. I hadn't finished painting until late and used this as an excuse to phone David to tell him I wasn't coming back. He wasn't happy and wanted to pick me up. I said no, convinced him I'd be fine, and reminded him that there was a police car outside. I would have gone back if it was any other time, but I had a plan that I needed to see through, and I didn't want to do it near his home. Where was Umbra?

Yawning non-stop and wondering why caffeine no longer affected me while I drank my fifth cup, I stepped away from my window and gave up my search for the night. I'd see her tomorrow. Hopefully.

I turned off the light and heard a hiss from behind. My heart pounded. I'd forgotten that she could go wherever she pleased. She had known I hadn't been here all week, instinctively knew not to come into David's home.

"I wondered when you'd show," I acknowledged.

Bowen and David had been right; she was creepy. Funny how I didn't feel that way as a child. With only the streetlamps offering light, I could see her perfectly, sitting in the middle of my living room. Her tail curled around her front paws, and she had my eyes; she was my creation, after all. Her head tilted in that peculiar way, as if she was studying me, perhaps gathering information to take back to the Inner Temple.

My hand shook as I reached into my back pocket, missing the opening several times. The music started downstairs. Really? Had the police spoken to them already? Well, that was fine; I needed them home for this to work anyway. They turned up the volume, giving me the strength, I needed to steady my hand and see this through.

Down on one knee, I sandwiched the two coins together. My heart was beating faster than the rhythm of the music. Umbra walked over to me, not a care in the world.

"I will continue the story tonight," I told her, feeling stupid for talking to this cat, but unlike others, I knew that she could understand me perfectly.

She looked up at me curiously, purred, and tilted her head again. Then, like a light switch, she pounced forward and snatched the coins from my fingers with her teeth.

"Ow, you little bitch," I snapped. I looked down and saw blood on my thumb and forefinger. "I created you. I can destroy you. You might want to remember that."

Maybe I wasn't as in control of this agreement as I thought. It was too late now. I watched Umbra walk off into the shadows and felt her presence fade to nothing. I just needed to word my next chapter carefully. Why did she have to show up so late? It was two thirty in the morning. This would take me a while. I could do it tomorrow, put work first, get some sleep. The music downstairs told me that wouldn't be happening any time soon. I went back over to my window and noticed that the police car was gone. I could call them back. Maybe Sally would. I sighed. This was exactly why I had to do what was needed to be done.

While the kettle boiled, I turned my laptop on and got comfortable. Right, what was it that I needed to remember... I'd remember while I typed...

...Ivy stood on the bank of the river Styx, awaiting the Ferryman. Through the falling ash she could hear his long oar being pushed into the riverbed. For many years, her people had stood on these banks, hoping to bargain with the Ferryman. He never came. She looked down at the coins in her palm; a beacon.

"He comes," her father said. "Daughter, do you remember what I told you? You are not to look directly at the Ferryman. You will place one coin into his hand before you step on to the boat. Keep your eyes on the current until you reach the other side."

"I understand," she said, keeping her voice steady. Her people, the eighty-two vampires left in existence, were watching in amazement and encouragement. This mission was one of desperation. She must succeed.

"Once you reach the other side, Umbra will be your guide through the Hellfire Caves. When you get to the Banqueting Hall, search for a skull carved into the stone. Place your hand over it and say... 'In jest she hid in an old oak chest. A dreadful doom as she waits in her tomb'. You will walk through the stone wall and find yourself in Minster Lovell Hall. The Mistletoe Bride will greet you and lift her left foot. Do you still have the coin?"

"Of course, Father."

"Varik has something for you." He waved him over.

"My queen," he said, while reaching into his cloak. "These are called sunglasses."

"I know what they are." Ivy snatched them from his hand and studied them. She unfolded the arms then folded them again, embarrassed that he'd given them to her in front of her people. Arthur, noticing her discomfort, took them from her and placed them on her face and over her ears.

"They won't stop the sun from blinding your eyes, just give them time to adjust." He leant down and whispered...

I put the kettle on again, then flipped it off. I could finish this tomorrow. Even though the party downstairs had gotten busier, louder, I could still sleep, have an okay day at work tomorrow. Or I could just have this circling in my mind all day. No, I will finish this. I grabbed a Coke from the fridge and a teaspoon from the draw. I scooped up a massive spoonful of coffee granules, put it in my mouth, then washed it down with diet Coke. A trick I learnt from one of my favourite horror films.

I must finish this…

...Ivy stepped into the shallow current, keeping her head down. She held her hand out for the Ferryman. When she heard the coin tap on his bone hand, she let go and stepped on to the boat.

Her people applauded and cheered. Ivy did not glance back; she did not want the images of their hopeful faces imprinted in her mind and heart. Instead, she nervously fiddled with the bag Hazel had given her. It held two thousand pounds of paper currency, a map of Witney and a Nokia mobile phone with its charger, not that she would have any use for it. Hazel and Willow had tried desperately to teach her how to use it; they said that it would have been easier if it hadn't run out of battery.

Her father had put a small photo of himself and her mother in her bag. A photo taken before their imprisonment. This angered her.

"You don't expect me to succeed, do you?" Ivy had said to her father.

"Daughter. I do expect you to succeed, you have no choice. The demons are very few, our people are starving." Running a hand through his thick black hair, he added, "Listen, Umbra has shown us much of the Watcher, but all we see is just a human. She's either a very powerful one, which I doubt, or something else entirely. When she said with conviction that she had created us and that she could destroy us, I felt fear for you."

"You fear nothing, Father. If she looked like a human, she will die like one, if it comes to that," Ivy said arrogantly.

"Fear will keep you alive, so fear you will. You will need her to provide more coins, and you will be wary of her. The world has changed much. Stay vigilant," he said, putting his hands on her shoulders. He leant down and kissed the top of her head.

The boat hit the bank, bringing Ivy back to the

present. Being mindful to keep her head down, she stepped off. She had been so deep in thought that she hadn't noticed the absence of ash. Her beloved ash. She hated this place already.

Umbra stepped from the shadows, green eyes staring intently.

"Show me the way, sweet Umbra," Ivy said, while running her fingers through her silky coat. "I'm thirsty."

Pain shot through my spine when my alarm went off. I had fallen asleep at my table again, using my keyboard as a pillow. What an idiot. I stood abruptly, sending the pain down my legs. At least I wouldn't be late for work. Had I completed the chapter? I thought so. Had I added as much detail as possible to get only what I wanted from this? Yeah, probably. I'd read over it later when I had time.

***

"You look rotten this morning," Rob said jokingly. Then seriously, almost worryingly, he asked, "Are you up for working today?"

I didn't blame him; all week he had been looking over my shoulder, making sure I had listened to my clients. It kept me on my toes. I had also cancelled my therapy session so that I could work the whole day when Rob needed me, hoping to make up for my mistakes. Both Olivia and Patch pretended that it never happened. I appreciated that too.

"I went back home last night, helped my neighbour Sally paint the hallway. It got late so I stayed. The party downstairs started when the police left, so I didn't get much sleep, but I'll be fine today, I promise."

"I thought you were going to stay at David's until they left," he said, frowning.

"I am. It was just one night. Plus, I don't think they'll be around for much longer." I smiled. Soon, if everything worked out, I would get my quiet life back. I had wondered, as I walked past their door this morning. I heard nothing, although, that wasn't unusual at that time in the morning.

"Ah, they're being evicted soon, that's good news." He clapped his hands together. "Chop chop, Zoe, get to work. These clients can't cut their own hair, although some of them bloody think they can." He laughed at his own joke.

The day went by quickly, which was a blessing. I was both shattered and desperate to read what I had written. Did Ivy threaten to kill me? No, I wouldn't have thought so. I might have forgotten a few details, but all should be good.

I smiled to myself when I remembered looking into the mirror first thing this morning and seeing little squares dented into my skin. I hadn't expected that. I also noticed my eyes; they looked different, brighter maybe, a deeper green. The dark circles were turning black now, blending into my pale skin. I looked different. Rob might have thought I looked rotten, but I liked my new look.

"Hi Zoe."

I looked up while sweeping my last client's hair away. Oh no.

"Hi Bowen. Rob won't be long, take a seat," I said shyly.

"Can… you do it?" he asked slowly, then grinned at me.

"Er, yeah. Come over." I looked over at Olivia and she gave me a sly smile. My hands trembled a little when I put the gown round him. He looked just as lovely out of his uniform as he did in it. He wore dark grey jeans without rips, a designer hoodie, and black Vans similar to mine.

"Hey Bowen," Rob called over the top of his client's

head. "She'll cut your ear off if you're not careful," he joked.

"Harsh, Rob," he laughed, then looked at me. "You won't, will you?" He was pretending to be nervous.

"I will if you tell me you don't like your haircut," I said then cringed. It sounded better in my head. I smiled and tried to remain professional. "What are we doing, a two back and sides?"

"Yeah, that's the one. How's your week been?"

"It's been good. I went home last night for the first time, but it's really not worth it until they leave. I take it they haven't been charged." I turned my clippers on, almost forgetting to put a guard on it. Focus. Focus.

"They're blaming their friends. It's hard to prove otherwise. They will leave soon enough. They can't live there without paying rent, but unfortunately it takes a while, something to do with the tenancy agreement."

"I know, Gary had explained it to me." I wanted to change the subject. "So, do you have much planned for today?"

"Just a few odd jobs. What about you, other than working here and trying to sleep, what else do you get up to?"

The unexpected question threw me off balance; it was normally us doing the asking. If it did happen and a client asked us something personal, we would answer it with another question.

"Not a lot. What do you do when you're not arresting arseholes?" I instantly blushed. Oh great, he'd think I was a potty mouth.

"When I'm not arresting arseholes," he smiled, "I go to the gym, I cycle, play football. I noticed you had a lot of books in your home."

"David owns a second-hand bookshop," I said weakly.

I put the clippers down and started combing his hair into sections. My hands shook a little. I was sure he noticed.

"You read a lot then? I noticed a laptop on your table and a load of notebooks. Are you studying for something?"

"What are you, a policeman?" I grinned. This felt like an interrogation. I smiled to myself and wondered why he was asking.

"You're very secretive," he grinned back. Then he raised his eyebrows, looking ready to take on a challenge. "Do you go to the pub or the cinema?"

"No. I just go home, read, write. Very boring," I said, realising for the first time just how tedious my life was. How lovely it would be to have a boyfriend, someone I could do things with, go places with. Maybe if he were mine, I'd watch him play football. Go on holiday. Go out and eat food other than beans on toast.

"Where do you go when you go out with your mates?"

I blushed and my heart sank at his innocent question. What mates? I never could make friends easily. My mum moved us around a lot, which meant I changed schools a lot. After David left, we moved away for a few years, then luckily, we moved back, because if we hadn't, I might not even have had him in my life. As for not having friends in my adult life, well, I didn't know why. Lucy called it 'fear of rejection'. She could be right.

"I go to book fairs with David sometimes," I blurted out, and hoped he didn't pry. He didn't, but just before he answered he gave me a sympathetic look. I hated it.

"Ah, cool. Well, I'm not just a sports fanatic. I loved dinosaurs as a kid and I still do. I have a couple of books about them, or did have." He beamed at me.

Why was he telling me this? I felt confused. Was he trying to connect with me?

"Yeah, I too have a few books on them. They're fascinating." Did he see them on my bookshelf?

"We could go to the Oxford Natural History Museum this weekend, if you want? I'm off this Sunday," he said casually.

Was he asking me out?

"Me?" I stupidly pointed to myself. I could hardly believe what I was hearing. My cheeks reddened.

"Yeah, you." He grinned. "I could pick you up at eleven."

I glanced around nervously and caught Rob's tight-lipped smile in his mirror, then, using my mirror, I glanced at Olivia and Patch. They'd all stopped talking to their clients. They were listening. Bowen either hadn't noticed or didn't seem bothered.

"She'll meet you at eleven. Won't you, Zoe?" Olivia called from behind me. I glanced up and saw her nod encouragingly at me.

I couldn't find my words, so I just looked at Bowen over his head through my mirror and nodded.

CHAPTER 7

Sitting opposite David brought home the reality of what I had done, or potentially done. I was still not entirely certain that everything would go to plan, and knew now that I hadn't really thought it all through. I still hadn't read what I wrote last night. A small part of me didn't want to know. I just wanted to put it in the back of my mind, forget about it. Everyone kept saying that the neighbours would be gone soon. Maybe they would have, maybe they wouldn't. Either way, I should have waited.

All I wanted to think about was what I'd be wearing on Sunday, but now I needed to mentally prepare myself.

Would there be a rotting body smell? If so, then how long would it take for the stench to creep through their door? Who would find the bodies? Would we all be investigated by the police? Probably not a good time to agree to spending the day with one. Funny how I didn't even give it a second thought when he was sitting in my chair. When the time came, would it be Bowen who interviews me, asking me where I was at the time of their deaths? My heart quickened. Would I be able to lie, and pretend to know nothing? Did my neighbours below have family? I didn't care at the time. I'd have to stay away until the bodies were discovered.

"Zoe, hellooo. Anyone home?"

"Sorry. What did you say?" I snapped out of my thoughts.

"I asked how your day at work was. Are you okay, poppet?" He was frowning at me.

"Yeah, I had a good day. Bowen asked me to go with him to the Natural History Museum this weekend," I said. This would keep my mind off things.

"Who is Bowen?" he asked, before putting a forkful of spaghetti hoops on toast in his mouth. It was my turn to cook tonight and I fancied a change.

"The police officer who dealt with the fire and…" I was still unable to talk about Goodboy and that night. "And he's a client."

"Why a museum, is that the latest thing?" He smirked.

"I'm not sure. It takes the awkwardness out of it though, doesn't it? I don't think I'd like some romantic meal out somewhere, too much pressure." I'd never been out to a romantic meal before; the thought of it filled me with dread.

"Smart lad," he approved. "Things are starting to look up for you now."

"I don't know why he asked me. What he sees in me." I felt my voice tremble, then from nowhere I started to cry. Why would someone as lovely as him want me, and why now? How would he feel if he knew the truth? I shouldn't have agreed to this. I could still cancel.

"Hey, hey now, poppet," he said, standing up to walk over to me. He pulled me up by my shoulders and cupped my face. "Zoe, you are a beautiful girl… a young lady. You're smart, kind-hearted. Everyone who knows you has wonderful things to say. You think I don't know about you sending your clients to my shop? They all say what a lovely girl you are. You're determined, too. Not a lot of girls your age could have bought a home. I was really proud of you that day, when you got your keys." He looked heartbroken for me.

"You helped me." I sniffed.

"No, I didn't, I didn't have the money, and your mother never helped you. The way she just moved to France like that. You were only eighteen. You soon got back on your feet though, didn't you? And rented that room. Then you worked two jobs to get where you are now. All I did was help you with the paperwork both times."

"Yeah," was all I could manage. They were hard times back then, and probably another reason why I didn't have any friends. I hadn't had time.

"Listen. I'll never know why you decided to walk into my shop that day, but I'm glad you did. You were my daughter back when I was with your mum, and you are now. Do you understand what I'm saying? You can tell me anything."

"David?" Guilt slammed into me full force for deceiving him. Had I lied directly? No. Would he find out what I did? Probably, if all went to plan. I looked down at the cuts on my thumb and forefinger from Umbra's bite. David noticed and frowned. He pulled my hand up to have a closer look.

"How did you get those? Did you cut yourself at work again?"

The first of many lies was on the tip of my tongue. As I looked into his patient blue eyes, guilt rippled through me. How could I have done this to him? He didn't have to take me in; he had no obligation to me. Would I lose him if I lied and he found out? Would I lose him anyway if I told him the truth? He was all I had, my only family.

"I'm sorry," I sobbed. What had I done?

"Sorry for what? For not listening to me?" he said simply. He was still holding on to my hand.

"What?" I stopped crying.

"Do you think I'm stupid? You've been acting strange all week, almost relaxed. That fire should have angered you, should have motivated you to seek justice. Instead, you were very calm, told me that you weren't surprised. Surprised or not, you didn't act like most people in your situation would have," he said, looking at me for my response. He too was acting unusually calm, considering my actions.

"I'm sorry." Would he ask me to leave?

"What's done is done, and you're going to have to live with it. You need to tell me everything. How many vampires are out? When are they coming?" His tone was authoritative.

"Just Ivy. She only has two coins. Umbra took them last night," I said, sniffing back my tears, looking down again at cuts from her teeth.

"What does she look like?"

"Like me, I suppose, green eyes, long dark hair. I didn't really describe her looks in my story."

"And what will she do once she's… what, eaten them, drank them? Maybe she'll play with them before she kills them?" he snapped, making me flinch. "Ah, you didn't think of that, did you?"

"No, I didn't." My heart thumped wildly. "She will go back home; she won't be able to use the internet to get more coins."

"Are you certain?" He rubbed his hand down his face. "And what of the bodies? They will start to rot, to smell. Who will find their bodies?"

"I could call the letting agency, tell them that there hasn't been anyone home, tell them that perhaps they've moved on."

"And let them find the bodies?" His eyes widened.

"It's what they deserve. They had plenty of opportunities to help us," I said bitterly. I meant it.

"Piss-poor attitude, Zoe. That being said, yeah, it would be better if they find them than anyone else, I suppose. You told me yourself that there won't be a typical vampire bite mark, you said 'mauled'." He paused. "When the police investigate, and they will, they may come to the conclusion that an animal had done it, but what animal and how did it get in?" He appeared to be talking to himself now. I watched him as he weaved around his piles of books without tripping.

"Their friends had dogs too, maybe—"

He shushed me.

"Their friend will be investigated. What if one of them doesn't have an alibi, will you feel guilty for sending an innocent person to prison?" He shook his head at me. "Don't answer that."

He stopped pacing and we both said nothing for a few minutes. He was thinking about something, and I was desperately trying to read his mind.

"Why aren't you angry at me?" I asked quietly.

"I'm furious with you, but as I said, what's done is done. We need to see this through and put it behind us."

He kept saying 'us' and 'we', making me believe that I hadn't lost him. A small part of me was glad that he knew. I didn't have to lie to him, and I had someone to confide in. I knew this was selfish.

"How did she get here from the Hellfire Caves so quickly?" he asked curiously.

"Can you remember taking me to the Minster Lovell ruins when I was a kid?"

He nodded.

"Can you remember the story you told me about the Mistletoe Bride?"

Another nod yes, then he shook his head in disbelief.

"I created another gateway. I linked the Minster ruins to the Hellfire caves."

"Just like that." He looked impressed, but only for a moment.

"Yeah."

"At least when the police do investigate you, you can say you've been here all week."

"Well, I wasn't, was I? She may have come early that morning, when I stayed that one night." I really hadn't thought this through.

"Okay. Well, if you do crack under pressure and admit to everything, about how you can write and create characters into existence, and then get them to do your bidding, then at the very most you'll be laughed out of the interrogation room."

***

The last couple days went by slowly. After we both read what I had written, we were horrified to learn that Ivy wanted to find me for more coins. David had said that I was not to return to my flat, but at the same time I needed to act as normal as possible. I needed to pick up some clothes from mine. He agreed, but only if he could come up with me. I saw Sally's curtain move while we were parked out front.

"Sally will notice you and might think that it's odd," I warned.

"How will she see me if I wait in your flat while you speak to her?"

"Trust me, she sees everything."

"Okay. Tell her, if she asks, that I needed to use your toilet."

We took the stairs slowly to the neighbours' door. If Gary was looking through his spyhole, then at least we could be honest and just say we were listening out to see if they'd left. He'd probably already done it himself. I put my ear flat against the door. Nothing unusual; they were usually asleep by now anyway, that's if they were still alive. Lifting up their letterbox brought sorrow to my heart, reminding me of Goodboy and the horrors that were done to him behind that door. I smelt nothing. Well, that wasn't true. I smelt stale smoke and sweat and a bin that needed to be put out. David stuck his nose in to smell too. He looked at me and shook his head.

I then knocked on Gary's door to tell him I was still staying at David's, and got no answer. Maybe he was still with his brother.

On Sally's and my floor, I couldn't help but notice how lovely and fresh the hallway looked before I snuck David into my flat. Then I knocked on her door with a pounding heart.

"Hi Zoe," she said while unlocking her door. She must have seen me through her spyhole.

"Hi, how have you been?" I asked cheerily. My real unspoken question was 'what do you know?' and 'what have you heard or not heard?'

"I've been very good. Who's that man with you?" she asked.

Amazing.

"That's David, he needed the toilet," I blurted out.

"I'd like to meet him," she offered. "Good news, those idiots downstairs have finally moved out – or done a runner, I should say. Their car is gone too. It's been great, peaceful.

I have told the letting agency, and told them to get their arses here and change the locks." She smiled. A real honest, happy, relaxed smile. She looked ten years younger already.

"When do you think they'll come?" My real question was 'how much longer do I need to hide away?' Wait… wait. "You said their car has gone?" Strange. Where was the car?

"Who knows. Yeah, their car is gone. When are you coming back?"

"I'm not sure, maybe when their locks have been changed."

"They've definitely gone," she said, trying to convince me.

"That's strange that they would just leave, they might come back," I said mechanically. Lying was not my strength. Hopefully David was right; when I cracked under pressure, and I probably would, I will just be laughed at.

"Not really. They owed a lot of rent. Can you imagine what state they've left that flat in?" she said, amused. The old Sally was back.

"Yeah, probably. I knocked on Gary's door. Has he been back?"

"He's been gone all week, I think. I thought I heard him down there a few times, but every time I went down to see him, I didn't get an answer," she said, frowning. "Where's David? I'd like to meet him."

"I'll go get him. Sally, could I give you my number so that you can let me know if anything happens?" This will give me time to prepare myself.

***

Tracing my hand over the triceratops's skull while Bowen read the plaque filled me with warmth. This was what regular people did. I'd had so much anxiety the previous night that I had barely slept. Nothing new, my mind and body was used to going without regular sleep. The people around me were used to my constant yawning. I had already apologised to Bowen for it and assured him it wasn't him. He said that it was understandable and put it down to me being under a lot of stress.

He was right.

"So… you had a good week?" he asked, unsure of himself. Our date had gotten off to an awkward start; we were both a little shy. This surprised me since he so confidently asked me to join him. We'd asked each other basic questions like 'what's your favourite film?', 'how old are you?' I was also surprised to learn that he was twenty-four, four years younger than me.

"It's been good, I'm still at David's. Sally thinks that the neighbours have moved out," I said, relieved that this was not a lie. She did in fact think that.

"Good, I'm glad to hear it." He smiled. "So, what is it that you write about?"

Oh, I hated it when people asked me this; it was why I never told anyone. Wait, how did he know?

"What do I write about?" I frowned.

"Yeah, you said that you go home, read, write."

"Ah, yeah. Just short stories. I enjoy it, keeps my mind busy. Maybe I'll do something with it one day," I said, feeling heat creep over my face as I looked down at the floor in an attempt to hide it.

I wanted to quickly change the subject before Bowen could ask me more about it. "Why did you move from Scotland?"

He'd probably been asked this question a thousand times.

"My grandma lives in Witney, I always visited as a kid and loved it. What are you writing about right now?" he asked, smiling slyly. He wasn't going to give up until I answered, was he?

"Umm… you'll think it's stupid."

"Try me."

"There are these caves in West Wycombe, called Hellfire Caves. Inside, there are many tunnels. Some believe that they are gateways, or portals if you like, to the underworld. I wrote a story about a vampire kingdom that is trapped within. They can't cross the boundaries to the human world because they can't access the gateway." I was unable to look up. It sounded so stupid saying it out loud.

"And will they get out?" he asked, sounding interested.

"I'm not sure yet." I told my first possible lie. "Where do you live?"

He smiled and accused me of being evasive. I didn't disagree.

"I actually live in the next village over, I lived with my grandma until I could afford to move out," he finally answered, taking pity on me.

"Do you have brothers, sisters?"

"Two brothers, and you?" He took my hand to lead me somewhere.

"I'm an only child," I answered absently, looking around at what he wanted me to see. We stopped in front of my favourite exhibit. "A plesiosaur?"

"Yeah, it's my favourite dinosaur," he said proudly. I couldn't help but smile; he was so wonderful. I looked down at his hand still holding mine.

"What?" He grinned at me.

"The Loch Ness monster is a plesiosaur. Is that why it's your favourite?" I laughed. It felt good.

"No, it's not," he said quickly. "Okay it is, but it's just a coincidence." He smiled shyly.

"It's cool though. Mary Anning used to excavate them from the Lyme coast," I rambled, and started to feel embarrassed again. He squeezed my hand and stepped in a little closer.

"Who is Mary Anning?" he asked softly, running his fingers through the front of my hair.

My heart pounded.

"She was a palaeontologist. Why did you ask me out?" I instantly regretted my stupid question. Not wanting to know the answer, I started to pull away. He took my other hand, stopping me, and pulled me closer to him.

"Because I think you're beautiful. When I saw you at Rob's, I'd hoped to see you again." He grinned at me. "Under different circumstances, though. After seeing you with Goodboy and being in your home, I knew that you were different from the girls I've met before."

I was unable to look down at my feet because he was standing so close. He curled a finger under my chin and lifted my face to meet his. Then kissed me.

***

After putting the phone down to Sally, I felt dumbfounded, my mind unable to process what she had told me. She had told me that the agency had come and changed the locks. Wendy, the owner, had been there too. Apparently, she had screamed when she saw the state of her property. Not that I cared about Wendy, not after what we had all been through. I had asked her if they found anything strange in the flat.

"Just a lot of rubbish, dog poo everywhere. All their clothes and furniture were left behind," she had said. Sally had also asked me for Gary's number, but I didn't have it. She told me she still hadn't seen him.

I laughed to myself. I laughed at both my foolishness and good luck. There were a number of reasons why this couldn't have worked. Firstly, I hadn't completed the chapter. Had Ivy given the Mistletoe Bride the sixpence? Was she still in the gateway, in between the Hellfire Caves and Minster Lovell? If not, did she get lost or feel so overwhelmed that she just went back? Secondly, and probably most obviously, was that I could not write characters into existence. Maybe when I was a child I could; that would explain Umbra, but not now.

My phone vibrated in my hand. It was a text from Bowen, asking me how my day at work had been. It hadn't been a good day, but I wouldn't be texting back that.

My concentration at work had been hit and miss. I had three more complaints, and Rob was at the end of his tether.

This could all be put behind me now; I could pretend it never happened. David would be pleased when I told him. Hopefully we could have a laugh over it. No more worrying about the police asking me questions or about Bowen finding out. He wanted to see me again after our day out; which I could hardly believe. *It could be the start of something wonderful,* I thought. I could also move back into my own home and start sleeping through the night again. My work life would no longer suffer. Everything was going to be great from now on.

I texted Bowen back, telling him that I'd had a great day and that the neighbours had finally gone. I ended the text with two kisses and stretched back against David's sofa and shut my eyes. Sleep came to me almost instantly.

CHAPTER 8

Lucy accepted my apology for cancelling our last two appointments. We took off our shoes and left them at the door. I still didn't fully understand why we did this, but I guessed that it was another thing they wanted us to do to help us feel comfortable. She asked how I'd been and got straight to the point.

"Do you want to discuss why you cancelled?"

Do I tell her everything? That was what I was here for. She'd think I'd gone mad; maybe even suggest medication. Either way, I needed to get this off my chest. Start fresh. Things were looking up for me now.

"Well, the first time was because I messed up massively at work, and I needed to try and make up for it. The second time was because I'd thought I killed my neighbours," I said with a rueful smile.

She blinked at me a few times. "When you say you thought you killed them, do you mean… imagined, perhaps fantasised about killing them?" Lucy looked serious. If it were me sitting in her chair, I wouldn't have been able to keep a straight face.

"Both, I suppose. A couple of weeks ago their friends started a fire in the communal hallway, right next to our only exit. I had both wished and imagined them burning to death. Then I thought I had killed them." My tone sounded casual, which surprised me. Then I felt guilty. It's then that I realised that thinking it versus saying it out loud felt completely different. It put things into perspective. But I had been so angry back then, and it felt justified.

"Okay. That's natural. They had been pushing your buttons for some time."

"It is?" I frowned. I hadn't expected her response.

"Oh yeah, plenty of people in your situation would have felt the same way. But what did you mean by 'thought you killed them'?" She was studying me.

I studied her right back. Could I do this? My heart pounded and I started to sweat. It was all or nothing. I started with Umbra watching me from across the road when Goodboy was being taken away, to what my characters had named me in my own story. I told her about what David had recalled when I was younger, with the mermaids and witches, and being able to write characters into existence. I also told her about the coins I ordered from an auction site and placing them in Umbra's mouth, so that she could take them back to the Inner Temple.

I looked down at the cuts on my thumb and forefinger, almost gone.

"Ivy was supposed to kill my neighbours in exchange for the coins, but I realise now that it never happened," I said, sounding relieved.

Lucy just sat there, staring at me. I smiled awkwardly,

waiting for her to say something. I recrossed my crossed legs. Seconds felt like minutes.

"Okay. Let's break this down." She bent down to grab a pen and pad from her purse. "While you were under extreme stress, you believed that the vampires from your story had tried to make contact with you. No, wait… they had sensed you watching them, and… and… my conclusion is this. You were under stress when you believed that the characters from your book were real. When your neighbours moved out, relieving you of this stress, you realised that this was just a fantasy." She wrote furiously. "Correct?"

"That doesn't explain Umbra," I said. I still had the evidence of her existence scratched on my fingers.

"Have you seen Umbra since your neighbours moved out?"

"No, I haven't, but that doesn't explain how David had seen her when I was a child, after I started writing about her."

"Has he seen her recently?"

"No, but he remembered her," I said slightly louder, trying to put my point across.

She pushed her glasses back up her nose and made no attempt to answer.

"Bowen saw her too, he's a police officer," I blurted. Then I felt stupid for trying to add credibility to my story.

"Is it possible that it was just a regular cat he saw, a regular cat that you had seen on many occasions?" she asked patiently. "You told me she was in your house, had disappeared into the shadows. Could it be a possibility that you were just very tired, possibly dreamt about it?"

I knew that this was as far as I was going to get. I didn't need to push this further. David and I knew the truth. We had discussed it after I told him about the conversation

I'd had with Sally. Our conclusion was that this was just something I could do as a child.

"Yeah, it could have been a regular cat," I said slowly.

***

"What's this?" I frowned while tossing the unidentified object into the air and then catching it like a cricket ball.

David bent down to read the label below the shelf. "It's a pomegranate, put it back. We're in the wrong aisle."

David always said it was best to buy fruit from the tinned aisles because it lasted longer. He was right. A tin of peaches was his favourite and mine was pineapple.

"Do you have any idea what he likes to eat?"

After therapy I felt relieved that Lucy had been so understanding. I guess you can't always predict how someone is going to react. Maybe she'd heard wilder stories. Then I popped into David's shop to see what he wanted for lunch and to cover for him while he took Missy out for a wee. While waiting in the queue for a baguette, Bowen texted me to see if I was free tonight. I wanted to get back to my flat, having spent so long away, so I decided to invite him over for dinner. David had offered to come shopping with me after he closed the shop to help choose what to cook.

"We only had coffee at the museum, but he did mention that he doesn't eat meat." I smiled, thinking back to our date, and our kiss. It really was a perfect day.

"I know what to get," he said abruptly, snapping me out of my memory.

He took my shopping basket and we weaved in and out of the way of other shoppers to the frozen food aisle – an aisle that we were both more familiar with. He opened the freezer door and pulled out two pizzas.

"You can't go wrong with cheese and tomato," he boasted. "What about dessert?"

"I don't know."

"Get a tub of ice cream just in case."

"Okay. Shall I get a bottle of wine as well, or is that too much?"

"Ha. I don't think so. Can't you remember what happened after that book fair in Stratford-Upon-Avon? You had one glass of wine and fell asleep in the crook of your elbow. I couldn't bloody wake you and had to hold on to you while we walked to the car."

I laughed, remembering that day. That glass of wine really had gone straight to my head; it had made me so tired. Maybe I should drink more often.

"Are you nervous about tonight? You seem on edge considering how well your therapy session went." David was the only person who knew I saw Lucy. It was him who suggested I went.

"A little, but mainly about going home. It's going to feel strange, but at the same time I'm looking forward to it."

"Fed up with my sofa?" He grinned.

We joined the end of the queue.

"Yeah, I am. I am really grateful to you, though. Thank you for letting me stay."

"No problem, poppet. I enjoyed the company. Have to be honest with you, I'll be glad all your stuff will be gone, made my home look like a right tip. I couldn't find a thing." He winked.

***

With twenty minutes to spare before Bowen arrived, I went down one flight to knock on Gary's door. No answer. I cheekily opened his letterbox to peek through. The lights were off, but I could smell that his plugin air fresheners were still on. Then I knocked on Sally's door. No answer either. It must have been the first time since I moved in that I'd had the building to myself. It felt eerie.

Bowen pressed the doorbell downstairs and I buzzed him up. I quickly ran into my bathroom to check my hair then opened my door.

"Hey, are you okay?" He smiled.

"I'm good, come in." I was pleased to see that he took his shoes off without me having to ask. He came in and put a bag down. I heard a clunk.

"I hope you don't mind but I brought beers and a bottle of wine for you. I wasn't sure if you drank, or what you drank if you did. I can only have one though," he said quickly.

I was pleased that he seemed as nervous as I felt.

"The wine's probably too strong for me, but I'll have a beer with you," I offered. *I will drink that slowly,* I told myself. We made our way into the living room, and I took his beers and put them in my fridge. It felt strange having him in my home under different circumstances. Actually, it was just strange. I had never invited anyone over before.

"How does it feel being back?" he asked, then took a seat on my sofa.

"Strange, but I'll be glad to be back in my own bed. I was staying on the sofa at David's because he's only got a one bed."

"It's all over now, you must be pleased. Do you have any idea where they went?" He nodded his head towards my floor to indicate the neighbours below. "We still have a few more questions for them. And when the vet, the one who is dealing with Goodboy's case, finishes with her report, they will be charged with animal cruelty."

I was pleased that Goodboy would be getting some sort of justice. Although, in my eyes, it would never be enough for what they did to him.

"Umm, no, no idea. Sally just told me that the letting agency came to change the locks. She said that they left everything behind. I think Wendy, the owner, will have to pay to have it all removed. Don't you think that's weird though?" I frowned.

"What's weird?"

"That they left all their stuff behind."

"Not really, we've seen this before. They were in a lot of trouble and didn't have time to move out. We'll find them eventually."

"They did take the car, so maybe they did take some stuff."

"No, they didn't have a car. It got reported then seized. No insurance."

Something niggled at the back of my mind, but I pushed it back, not wanting to think about it. Enough talk of them downstairs, it was behind me now. The car meant nothing.

"I got us pizzas, I hope that's okay," I said shyly. This would be the first time I had made dinner for someone.

"My favourite." He stood and walked over towards my table. "What are you working on now?" He ran his finger over my laptop. His eyes flickered over my notebooks.

I had been working on something. Now that I had free rein to write what I wanted and didn't have to worry about vampires being unleashed into the world, I had gone a little mad. I wanted to delete the last story, chapter at a time, but when I got to Varik and Goodboy's part, I didn't have the heart. I changed it to only them being trapped, the last two survivors. Ivy, Arthur, Hazel and Willow no longer existed. I took away the ash and gave them a sun that neither set nor rose, hidden behind a thin layer of cloud to protect Varik's eyes. At the last second, I recreated Goodboy. He, like Umbra, was now a phantom, who had died in the human realm and had been resurrected in the afterlife. He will be able to cross boundaries at will. I had planned to revisit their story one day, but not yet. Then I started a new page.

"I could show you if you want," I said, instantly regretting it. I sat down at the table and fired up my laptop. "It's just the start, nothing great yet."

Cretaceous Coast

Wind slapped against Harry's plastic bag as he bent down to pick up another empty bottle. He was both disgusted and annoyed at the way people could just throw their rubbish on these beautiful scenic shores. He shook his head, unable to understand it. A lot of the plastic bottles could be found only metres away from the bins provided.

Hearing a loud splash, he stood tall, looking out at a large circular ripple in the usually calm waters. He watched, mesmerised as the ripples slowly blended into the soft ocean waves. Then further across he saw something breach the surface...

"Ah, you're writing about Nessy, aren't you?" He grinned at me; his eyes were bright with affection.

"Well, sort of. Plesiosaurs are marine reptiles. My version of Nessy will live in the ocean off the coast of Scotland. I'm not sure which coast yet. I'll need to do a little more research."

He nodded his head approvingly. "Sounds interesting."

I could feel myself blushing. "I'll write about more than just one. Maybe a pod."

"A pod?"

"If a family of whales is called a pod, what's a family of marine reptiles called? I really need to do a lot of research before I continue." I shifted uncomfortably in my chair, feeling awkward. I hadn't shared what I had written with anyone but David. I might have told Lucy, but never showed her. I was unable to read his mind as he carried on reading.

"I'll put the pizzas on."

"Okay," he said, not taking his eyes off the screen.

I read the instructions for the third time, not wanting to mess this up. Preheat the oven, twenty minutes. Simple.

"It's really good. I like that you're changing the legend slightly. Will you let me read the rest when it's done?" he asked.

"Yeah, of course," I said quietly, blushing again at his compliment.

***

After our dinner we sat on the sofa with a film on in the background. We barely glanced at it. He was so easy to talk to and I became more and more comfortable as the night went on. And I hadn't spaced out once. When he stood up to leave, I walked with him to the door.

"Thank you for inviting me over," he said, as he stepped closer to me.

"That's okay, it was nice." I stepped into his arms. We kissed more passionately than at the museum; more sensual, our breathing heavier. He gently backed me against the door, leaning his body into mine, then ran his hand over my hip while my fingers stroked his jaw. He left my lips to trail warm kisses down my neck to my chest while he used both his hands to push my breasts up. Before I was aware of what my hands were doing, they had slipped under his shirt. His body felt hard and smooth. Athletic.

"I could stay the night, if you wanted me to?" he whispered in my ear, sending chills throughout my body.

"I'd like that," I whispered back.

***

I was gently being shook as I woke. At first, I was unaware of my surroundings. Was it Missy needing a wee? Then all of a sudden, she said, "Zoe?"

"Missy?" I slurred, then fear beat through my heart, sending me bolt upright in bed. A scream lodged in my throat.

"No. It's Bowen," he laughed. "Did you think I was someone else? I'm glad you said a girl's name and not some bloke's."

"I thought you were Missy." I rubbed my eyes, trying to see him, but it was pitch black. "David's dog."

"You thought I was a dog?" he teased.

I giggled. "Yeah, sorry. Are you okay?" It was then that I realised that he was kneeling by the side of my bed.

"I'm being called into work early; they've found something that needs all hands on deck. I didn't just want to leave without saying goodbye."

"What's the time?"

"It's four in the morning. I'll text you later, okay?"

"Okay. Did you want to use my shower?"

"No, that's alright. I need to go home and get a change of clothes anyway."

He kissed me then quietly left, opening then gently closing my door. Then the door reopened.

"Did you want to lock the door behind me, just in case?"

I felt warmth towards him for being so considerate. I walked to the door, feeling excited at being able to kiss him one more time before he left.

"Bye," he whispered, giving me another kiss.

"Bye."

I closed the door and leant against it, smiling, thinking about the night before. It had been wonderful; he was wonderful. I felt wide awake and decided to stay up and make a coffee. I sat at my table and started to write. My morning alarm would tell me when it was time to stop and get ready for work.

Three hours later and as usual I was shocked at where the time went. I made another coffee and stared out over my beautiful view. The sun was out, the day was going to be great.

While I was locking my door, I heard Sally open hers.

"Morning," she beamed.

"Morning, Sally. I knocked on your door last night. I wanted to know if you'd heard anything else." I knew that she would have.

"I was out with my hubby last night. We had a lot to discuss. I saw a car parked in your space when I got back. Did you have company?" she asked nosily. *Unbelievable*, I thought, then smirked.

"Yeah, I had company. Have you heard from Gary?"

"It's so strange, I heard a woman's voice down there a couple of times, so I know he's home, but he never answers." She frowned.

"Maybe he has a new lady friend, doesn't want to be disturbed," I suggested. Not that Sally would care about disturbing someone.

"Well, you could be right. I thought it was a woman's voice coming from his television. Wendy is coming back today to start with the clean-up downstairs. You should have seen it in there." She shook her head while grinning. "I don't envy her."

"Neither do I," I said honestly. I had been a bit harsh towards Wendy, but I realised that it wasn't her fault. She didn't choose the tenants. I said my goodbyes then started my walk to work.

***

Everyone, including the clients, had been very excited at the barber shop. They were talking and gossiping about what could have happened to have three roads closed off by the police in town. How sad. But that's what happened when you lived in such a quiet town; you got excited about road closures.

"My friend told me it was a rape, someone walking back late at night," Patch's client said.

Olivia's client had said it was a hit-and-run. One of mine tried to convince me that it was a robbery gone wrong.

"Maybe it's a murder," Rob suggested, getting caught up in the gossip.

I guessed that this was the reason why Bowen had been called to work early. I could ask him, but I didn't want to pry or come across as nosy. As much as I loved Sally, I didn't want to be like her. He'll either tell me or he won't, I decided.

It was close to closing time and I still hadn't heard from him. Should I text? I wouldn't phone him just in case he was still working.

"How's things going with you and Bowen?" Olivia grinned at me.

Just as I was about to answer, he walked through the door. My heart quickened. He shook hands with Rob and nodded to Patch and Olivia. He looked over to me to say something when Rob cut him off. "Why are the roads closed, what happened?"

I cringed.

"I can't discuss information on an ongoing case," he said curtly. "How's business been today?" he asked, keeping the conversation light.

Rob nodded his head in understanding. "It's been good, busy." Then he went back to cashing up.

I walked over to him. He looked tired, not his usual contented self. "Are you okay?"

He nodded. "I'll drive you home tonight. You were headed straight home, weren't you?"

"Yeah, I'll go grab my stuff," I said slowly.

Something was off. My first thought was that he regretted last night, then I felt stupid and selfish. He'd obviously had a tough day at work; this had nothing to do with me. But why was he here?

We walked to his car in silence. When we got in, he faced me, then opened his mouth to say something, then stopped.

"Are you okay?" I asked again.

"Are you not going to ask me what happened?" his tone was sharp.

"No. It's none of my business," I mumbled.

He gave me a half smile. "Can you keep what I'm about to tell you to yourself?"

"You don't need to tell me anything." I shrugged. "It's police business."

"Well, I need to talk to someone about this, and I'm not going to tell my grandma, it will scare her."

"Is what happened the reason why you got called in early?"

He sighed heavily. "Yeah, it was."

I leant closer to him and stroked his hair back from his face, waiting for him to talk.

"I didn't see the body, just saw the blood smeared through the grass and my colleague throwing up on a gravestone." He paused. "Someone… a woman, a jogger, we believe, was found dead in the graveyard close to your home. It looked like an animal attack, too savage to be a dog. We're investigating the local zoo to see if any of their animals have escaped." He leant over his steering wheel, resting his forehead on his arms.

"Bloody hell, really?" Things like that never happened in our town.

"Yeah. I wanted to drive you home, it's not safe for you to walk back." He sighed heavily again. "I don't mean to sound forward, but would you mind if I came in for a bit?"

"Of course," I said while still stroking his hair. Something niggled at the back of my mind again, but I let it go. I didn't want to think about it.

CHAPTER 9

Bowen had stayed with me all week, apart from the times he worked nights. He insisted on picking me up and driving me home for my own safety. The news of the jogger had shocked and scared the people of Witney; all parents had been advised to pick up their children from school, and joggers told not to run through wooded areas and to run in pairs or more. A curfew had also been put in place, advising people not to leave their homes unless it was absolutely necessary to do so. The graveyard was still taped off, no visitors allowed until further notice; not that anyone would dare wander through.

All evidence pointed towards an animal attack, but the local zoo insisted that no animal had escaped. They were ordered to close for the day, to check all the enclosure perimeters for openings either made by the animals themselves or by someone who thought it would be entertaining to release a dangerous animal.

What happened to that jogger had affected Bowen. He

was struggling to sleep and had to do extra shifts. I was just glad to be there for him.

That niggle I had, came and went. What if?

I was sitting at my table, writing, when David texted, asking me to go to his shop tomorrow. 'Okay, no problem', I texted back. Strange; he didn't normally text. He hated it.

"Who was that?" Bowen asked.

"Nosy," I teased. "It was David. I'm going to go to his shop tomorrow after work."

"Will he drive you back after? I'll be working so I won't be able to pick you up." He sounded worried.

That part of me that wanted someone to want me was contented. His worrying for me was alien, yet it filled me with warmth.

"Yeah, I'm sure he will," I assured him. "This chapter's complete. Did you want to read it?"

I had been letting him read my stuff all week. I had enjoyed watching him smile while he read, and I enjoyed answering all his questions after he finished.

"Yeah." He got up and came over, but instead of taking the seat opposite, he pulled me up, sat in my chair, then pulled me down on his lap. I blushed and mentally took in every moment with him as if it were my last.

He kissed my neck while keeping his eyes on the screen.

"Whalers," he shouted, making me jump off his lap. "No, you can't do that. The plesiosaurs have only just been discovered. Would they really get hunted?"

I laughed, then went into the kitchen to make us a drink.

"Yeah, of course. In the name of science, they would be caught, dissected and studied. Hell, in the name of conservation they'd probably be captured and put into aquariums, just so people can gawk at them."

"You're not going to let that happen, are you?" He gave me a knowing look.

"I might, not sure yet." This made me feel powerful in a 'master of my own universe' kind of way. "Maybe Harry will do everything in his power to save them."

"I hope so."

***

Work had been manic all day and I was so relieved it was over; my legs were killing, and I didn't have time for lunch. I walked slowly to David's shop, thinking about what he wanted to talk about. Again, I felt that niggle, an unease. Why did he text instead of phone? I stood outside his shop with my hand on the handle, debating whether to go in or not. *This is stupid*, I told myself. I was overthinking things. I would either overthink things, or push it back and not think of it at all. It was fair to say that I pissed myself off sometimes.

"Hey David," I said, walking to the back of the shop while he served his last customer. I picked up a few books off the floor while I waited, then put them back down because there was nowhere else to put them.

"Poppet. Come here." He pulled me into a tight hug, then went over to the door to flip the open sign to closed, then locked it.

"Are you okay? I've been worried. You don't normally text." I frowned.

"I wasn't sure if you were with Bowen or not."

"I don't care about that. Actually, I'd like for you to meet him soon."

David ignored that and sat behind his desk. He pulled out a stool for me. He looked concerned, tired, then he looked at me as if he was waiting for me to say something, but it was him who invited me. I shrugged at him.

"What do you think about that jogger?" he started.

I started to feel uncomfortable. "I only know what Bowen has told me, and that's not much more than you know. Why?" I asked, confused. Why did he want to discuss the jogger?

"Do you really think an animal did it?" he asked, arching his brow.

Heat crept throughout my body, and I was unable to meet David's gaze. My heart sank. One night when I was alone in bed, I let those niggles from the back of my mind come to the surface. I loosely pieced together an alternative to what I thought I believed. What I wanted to believe. My life was good now, it was quiet. It was how it should always have been, and I wasn't going back.

"Yes, an animal did it. That's what the evidence suggests." My eyes started to water. Please stop talking, David.

"Any other possibilities? The attack was too savage to be a dog, and no animals escaped. So, what do you think happened to the jogger?" His face was unreadable.

"I don't know." I stood up and paced around the shop, pretending to look for a book. Then I turned toward him.

"I know what you're getting at. We both agreed that it didn't happen, that Lucy was partly right. I was under extreme stress and wasn't sleeping, and imagined the whole thing," I ranted. "You didn't help. You were the one that put it in my head."

"You're blaming me? That's rich. You're the one that came to me, asking me if I remembered that cat. I told you what I knew, that's all. Something you also knew, by the way. But you chose to put it to the back of your mind, as usual." His tone was sharp.

"What do you mean by that?" My anger flared, but it wasn't aimed at him. My world was about to come crashing down and there was nothing I could do to stop it. I felt like a deer in headlights that had no choice but to stand there and wait for the impact.

"When bad things happen to you, or things that you can't comprehend, you just bottle it up, pretend it never happened." He rubbed a hand down his face. "Look, I want to be wrong, I do, but what if it wasn't an animal attack?"

"It was, and that's final." My voice trembled.

"Where did your neighbours go?" He tried from a different angle.

"I don't know, they just moved on. If Ivy had done it there would have been bodies. Nothing was found," I said, not only trying to convince him, but myself also.

"I'm not trying to upset you. But hypothetically speaking, what if she killed your neighbours and hid the bodies? She'll be smart, right? She wouldn't want to get caught, not before she got those coins."

"David, please. Don't you understand what you're doing?" I snapped. "If Ivy killed them and that jogger… it will be… it will be my fault. I killed them," I sobbed. My whole body was shaking.

David stood and put his arms around me. "It's not your fault, it's not." He tried to soothe me. But he couldn't. The truth was out now.

"Why did you have to say something? Why couldn't you just let it go?"

"You knew too, you were thinking it. What were you going to do, just let the bodies pile up all over Witney?" He stepped back and looked at me. "We need to put a stop to it; we need to act fast before anyone else dies. We'll get your laptop and go through the story; we'll figure out a way to stop her."

My breathing slowed; he was saying 'we' again. "I deleted the story. Her home as she knows it is gone, and how will we convince her to go back without the coins anyway?" I would lose Bowen when the truth came out, but at least I'd always have David.

"We need to find her, then offer her more coins. I assumed she would have come to you by now." He shook his head, trying to dislodge the thought. "I'm glad she hasn't. Then when she goes back, you could permanently close the gateway."

"I don't think it works like that. I'd also need a reason to close the gateway." My thoughts flickered to Varik and Goodboy. I couldn't sacrifice them like that.

"Because in order for her to go back, the gateway must work, so to just take it away wouldn't be accurate. For your stories and characters to become real, it must be accurate." He frowned, trying to make sense of it.

But none of it made sense.

"Plus, even if I could close the gateway, we wouldn't know the exact moment she'd return. If she does go back, she will find out her father and people no longer exist. To her they will be dead. She will come straight back out looking for me," I croaked, tears streaming down my face again. I just deleted her family without a second thought. Why did I feel for Ivy? Was it because she was a part of me? All she really had was her father and her father's library, like me only having David and his bookshop.

"Okay, let me think." He pinched the bridge of his nose.

"She will have a similar personality to me. I might be able to reason with her."

"And say what? We'll have to kill her, Zoe, and it won't be murder because she doesn't really exist. Well, she does, but not naturally."

"How will I do it?" The thought made me feel sick.

"I will do it."

"No," I pleaded. "This is my mess; I will do it."

"I have no attachments to her; it will be easier if I do it." He gave me a tight-lipped smile.

There was no way I was going to let him do this. I would have to cross that bridge when I came to it. Anyway, could she have lasted this long in our world? She could have returned already and might not show again. Well, she wouldn't be able to with only one coin left.

"What do I tell Bowen?" My heart sank again. It was then that I realised something. I loved him and now I will lose him.

"Poppet, tell him nothing, he wouldn't understand. We will be able to see this through without anyone finding out," he assured me.

But I still had to live with this; we would both have to. The jogger's name was Amber Morris; she was thirty-five and lived and worked in town. She was someone's daughter, granddaughter, sister, niece. She had friends, a life, a boyfriend. Her photo had been shared on social media; she had been beautiful and looked full of life. But now she was just known as 'the jogger'.

***

My mind wondered back to the weekend while I was methodically sectioning off my client's hair. David had insisted that I stayed with him again, but I needed time to myself. Bowen had texted me asking if I had got home safely and if he could come over after work. I texted back saying that I had.

I wanted to tell him not to come over. How could I look at him knowing what I knew? What if he started talking about the case as he had done all week? Would I crumble? But I wanted to see him, wanted to make the most of him, knowing that my time with him was coming to an end.

We'd had the perfect day yesterday and it started with me waking up next to him. He wanted to make dinner for me, and I loved every moment of it, watching him cook in my kitchen. We shared a bottle of wine that went straight to my head, but it gave me the courage to suggest we had a bath together; he was more than happy to join me.

"EXCUSE ME!"

I snapped out of my memory. I looked down and saw that my client was glaring at me. Then I saw Rob standing behind me through my mirror.

"I wanted it cut shorter than that," my client said sharply.

"Oh, sorry. I can do that," I muttered. Realising that it wasn't anything too serious, Rob walked back to his station next to mine. I could feel his eyes on me.

I started sectioning off his hair again to cut it shorter. *Must keep my mind on the job*, I chanted to myself. I'd already be losing so much. Not knowing when I'd be losing everything was agonising, and not knowing how this was going to go down was worse. What if Ivy didn't show? Should I have just let bodies pile up around town, as David had put it? Should I come forward with the truth? I'd be laughed at and that's how I'd lose Bowen. I already knew that much. He'd think I was delusional. I felt my mind wondering again and looked over to Rob. He looked anxious while he watched me. Something caught my attention through his mirror. A black flicker. It was Umbra. That little bitch looked so content while she stared back at me. My heart didn't pound with fear this time; it was fury.

Crunch.

"Ow… Ow…"

My client bent forward, cupping his ear. He was howling. Blood dripped on to the white and black striped gown. He frantically used his other hand to get out of my chair to inspect his ear in the mirror.

Rob rushed over, trying to pull the client's hand back to see the damage.

"Patch. First aid kit. Now."

"I'm sorry… sorry." My scissors slipped off my fingers to the floor. I looked down and saw his blood on my trembling hand. The cut must have been deep.

My client looked bewildered. "What the fucking hell? You cut my ear. Rob? What the hell is this, what the—" He took his hand from his ear and looked at the blood.

"Clive. I'm incredibly sorry. Let me look." Rob was panicking. "Patch?"

Patch was standing behind Rob. He was frantically trying to open the first aid kit. Rob snatched it from him. When he opened it, everything inside spilled out, falling all over the floor.

Olivia rushed over and grabbed my arm. She led me to the staffroom.

"I think it's best if you stay out of the way." She gave me a sympathetic smile that I didn't deserve.

"I'm so sorry. I don't know what happened." But I did. Umbra was here.

"Rob's going to sack you after this. I'm not saying this to be cruel. Just prepare yourself, okay?"

"I know." I trembled.

"I'm sorry Zoe, but I can't wait in here with you, I have a client in my chair. But listen, a few years back Rob employed this guy called Stuart. He became an absolute liability because he was an alcoholic, and got sacked. A few months later, Rob gave him a second chance." Olivia gave me another sympathetic smile. "Leave now, and try to come back when you've sorted yourself out."

"Where's Stuart now? Did he cut someone's ear?" I must have been in shock before because now tears streamed down my face. Or maybe it was Olivia's kindness.

"He started drinking at work again and got sacked… again. No, he didn't cut anyone's ear. I'm sorry, but I need to go." She hugged me tight, then left.

Now that I was alone in the staffroom, I could hear what was going on in the shop.

"Patch? Drive Clive to the hospital—"

"No. I don't think so. I will go by myself," Clive snapped. "Someone needs to answer to this. I can't let her get away with this," he threatened.

And rightly so.

The front door slammed shut for the second time thanks to me, and I heard Patch and Rob talking quietly. I couldn't hear what they were saying, but I already knew. I washed the blood from my fingers then stood facing the door, waiting for Rob. My tears had already dried on my face. I was ready. I breathed in for five seconds, then released my breath for five seconds. I was calm.

The door opened gently. Rob, instead of looking furious, seemed sorrowful. "I wanted this to work out. I won't ask what happened because I don't want to hear your excuses."

"I know. I'm sorry." That was all I could say. It was probably all he'd accept, anyway.

"There's a bag under the sink. Put all your stuff in there and go." He calmly opened the door then walked out.

A small part of me was relieved that he didn't shout or get angry with me. I loved this barber shop and I didn't want the memory of this place to be completely tarnished. Then my mind swirled with frantic thoughts. I would have to tell David that I lost my job, again. Bowen would find out and start asking me questions that I just couldn't answer. If I couldn't find a job fast enough, I would have to sell my home. All because of my disgusting neighbours downstairs. My fury returned, but deep down I knew I only had myself to blame; I needed to accept that. I was told that they were getting evicted, but I just didn't believe it; seemed too good to be true, and I wanted them to pay for what they had done.

I wanted to blame them for losing Bowen, but I realised that if it hadn't been for them, I wouldn't have met him out of work. Maybe, eventually, he still would have asked me out while cutting his hair. I'd never know.

But most of all I wanted to blame them for the death of the jogger. If they hadn't pushed me to my limits, I wouldn't have done what I did. I felt like I had no choice, but I did. I could have just waited until they left.

I took one last look around the staffroom then went to clear my station. Patch was already there, unplugging my clippers and neck trimmers. Olivia spoke quietly to her client, without looking over, and Rob was nowhere to be seen. I had no doubt he was waiting for me to leave.

Patch helped me pack up the rest of my stuff. He picked up my scissors off the floor, grabbed a tissue from the box near the till, then wiped the blood off them before handing them back to me. I stared at them for a moment. I will never cut hair again.

"If it makes you feel any better, it was just a small nick. A lot of blood for a small nick, but he'll live." Then quietly he said, "And he was a prick, by the way. You couldn't have picked a better client to slice and dice than that one."

I gave him a tight-lipped smile.

I appreciated what he was trying to do, but it had gone too far; so much was on the line. I had to fix what I had done. I couldn't turn back the clock, but I could put a stop to Ivy before she killed anyone else. I needed to find her. Where was she?

***

Umbra followed me all the way home, and now that little bitch was watching me from outside, below my kitchen window. Like an idiot, I screamed and shouted abuse at her while walking back, and all I got in return was a lot of worried looks from people walking past. One woman even got her phone out, ready to film me. It wasn't every day you saw a mad woman shouting at the pavement, I supposed. I didn't care that no one else could see her; I was past control.

My phone rang. It was Bowen. I was about to switch my phone off when I realised, he could just turn up. I needed to be alone tonight, I needed to search for Ivy. Now must be the time. Why else would Umbra just show up?

I texted him telling him that I was okay, and that I needed time to myself.

He texted back, telling me he had dropped by Rob's earlier. He asked me why I wasn't at work and said that Rob had told him to ask me. That was kind of Rob; he didn't have to do that.

I wanted to be honest with him, so I replied saying that I had been sacked and that I needed time to myself. Then I sent another text pleading with him not to come over. I just hoped that he would listen.

He sent back a long text saying that he was there for me if I needed him. My tears blinded me, making it impossible to read the rest of the message.

I paced around my living room, waiting for the sun to go down. How would I find her? I thought I knew where she could be – the graveyard. It must be the graveyard; it was where she'd killed the jogger. No, I wouldn't call her 'the jogger'; she had a name. Amber Morris.

I couldn't give Ivy more coins, even as a bribe. She must also be prevented from getting more coins from a different source. I only had one choice. David had said it and I needed to accept it.

I rifled through my draws for a knife. It would need to be big and sharp enough to remove her head. I retched at the thought. Frantically, I tried to figure out a different way to kill her, knowing full well that when the time came, I wouldn't be able to follow through. I was not a killer. But I'd have to put things right.

I opened up my laptop and tried to find a way to weaken my vampires, but it was too late; she was already out. I couldn't change my characters once they were out.

I wrapped myself in a long coat and tucked a knife in my pocket. It wasn't big and it wasn't very sharp, but it was all I had; my only choice. I looked out my window one more time to see if Umbra was still watching. She was gone. I had thought that perhaps she was waiting for me, that she was going to lead me to Ivy. I was wrong. I felt frustrated at not knowing what her game was. She'd obviously just been watching me to show Ivy what I had been doing.

It was late when I gently opened my door so that Sally wouldn't hear. Then I started to creep down the stairs. As I passed Gary's door, I heard something uncanny. It was a one-sided conversation. The voice sounded similar to my own.

Realisation hit me like a car crashing into another. Oh no, how could I not have known? Why didn't I figure this out sooner? When was the last time Sally and I had heard from Gary? She was in there. He was dead, he had to be. I killed him. This was my fault.

I gasped, sucking in a huge breath of air. The one-sided conversation stopped abruptly. She must have been talking to Umbra.

I heard my heart pounding in my ears as I crept back up the stairs. An idea came to me. It might work. It came to me so quickly that I didn't have time to properly think it through, but I needed to act fast. I needed to act now.

In my kitchen cupboard were two large boxes of matches. One was half empty, but it would have to do. I crept back downstairs and quietly walked to Gary's door. I struck a match then quickly put it back in the box, igniting all the others. Then I put it through his letterbox, then did the same to the other box. I knew that it wouldn't start a fire, but hopefully the smoke would fill the air, setting off the fire alarm.

My plan was for the fire service to knock down Gary's door and find his body. I retched again, more so than at the thought of taking Ivy's head off. That bitch had what was coming to her now. Oh Gary. What had I done?

I waited for Gary's fire alarm to go off then I ran back upstairs and banged on Sally's door.

"Sally… Sally," I shouted. Oh shit, was she dead too? I panicked.

Her husband opened the door, surprising me. When did he come back?

"That's the fire alarm," he shouted behind his shoulder. "Sally, get up." Then he turned back to me, not noticing that I was already in my coat. He barked, "Get your coat and wait outside. Now."

I rushed through my door and grabbed my phone. Should I call in the emergency, or let Sally do it? The decision was made when I heard her husband on the phone to them in the communal hallway. My door already opened,

I saw Sally and walked down the stairs with her. Smoke was already filling the hallway outside Gary's door.

"It's Gary," Sally shrieked. "Oh my god. Open his door," she shouted to her husband. "Open it."

Her husband, while still on the phone, lightly touched the door handle. He told the operator what he was about to do, then stopped. He shook his head at Sally. "I can't, I've been told to wait."

"Gary, Gary," Sally shouted at the door.

"Come on," he said, pulling her down the next flight of stairs.

I opened the front door and we all spilled out and ran to the other side of the road to look in Gary's window. Nothing; no lights were on and no glow from a fire. The alarm could still be heard. Hopefully that was enough for the firefighters to knock his door down, although I suspected his door would be unlocked.

"Are you okay, Zoe?" She looked at me, up then down. "Why are you dressed?" She missed nothing.

I couldn't lie on the spot, so I stuttered, "I haven't been to bed yet." Half-truth. She accepted this then asked if I was okay again.

"Yeah, I'm okay."

The fire engines arrived and Sally's husband told us to stay put, then went off to talk to them.

"Poor Gary," Sally whispered to no one.

I stood there in silence, thinking about what to do next, and what would happen next. The firefighters entered the building.

Oh Gary, I'm so sorry. After this, I would have to come forward. I wouldn't even discuss it with David. I would just walk right into the police station and confess.

"Watcher."

I spun around to the voice that came from behind me. Nothing.

"Sally, did you say something?" I frowned.

"I said, I hope Gary is okay. Maybe he's not home. I bet one of his plug-in air fresheners caught fire." She was quick.

Sally's husband ran back over to us. "They're calling for medical assistance. He must have been home."

What? Could he have been alive? Relief flooded throughout my body.

Then I felt something rub against my leg, making my stomach churn. It was Umbra. I kicked her away, but my foot went straight through her. Of course; she could become intangible at will. She ran off up the road towards the bridge. I watched as she curled around the ankles of a woman in a black cloak. It was Ivy.

CHAPTER 10

Sally ran off into the building, leaving me standing in the street, gaping at Ivy. I wanted to avoid this, to put this in the back of my mind and move on, but I couldn't, not now. When I tried to walk towards her, I realised my legs wouldn't obey. I was still grounded. Hearing more sirens in the distance worried me. Could Bowen be with them? He was off shift but could have been called in. I panicked. Needing to avoid him, I walked up the bridge towards Ivy. My body felt numb.

Her long dark hair and cloak whipped with the wind. The moon illuminated her pale face. Her features were similar to mine but sharper, more regal. She was sneering at me, mocking me. She looked arrogant, just like the queen I had created.

A few metres away from her was close enough, yet far away enough from my building. The police cars and ambulance abruptly pulled up.

"Your army has arrived," she smirked. My green eyes in her face glowed with wickedness.

My army? She thought that they belonged to me. Why? Then I remembered that the first time she had seen me was with them. I tried my luck.

"Yeah, my army has arrived." My voice trembled.

"It matters little, they are just human, as are you, Watcher." She cocked her head to the side, studying me. "You will provide me with coins. Yes."

"No… no I can't. You have one coin… go back," I stuttered.

"I have been watching you, Watcher. What are you? Why do you think you created us?" She looked amused.

"Because I did."

She smirked at this and waved her hand, dismissing what I said. "Coins. Give them to me, or your familiar will starve to death, all over again."

Familiar? She was talking about Goodboy. How devious of her. I felt inward relief. No, Goodboy would not starve again. He was a phantom now and would never be a victim again. She obviously hadn't been back to the Inner Temple, or she would have known.

"Let him starve. You need to return," I said, trying to sound cold, but my trembling voice betrayed me.

She cocked her head to the side once again, this time smiling, revealing her double row of serrated teeth. My thoughts flashed to Gary.

"What did you do to Gary?"

"I do not answer to you, Watcher."

"What did—"

"You have a human male. I have heard you with him. His scent is alluring, is it not?" She grinned, once again revealing her teeth.

My heart hammered when I realised, she was talking about Bowen. I looked over my shoulder down the road to see the officers rushing in and out of my building.

"He is not down there," Ivy said.

"Leave him alone." I realised then that I had no choice but to give her what she wanted. "I don't have the coins on me, I had to order them online."

"That is what that pathetic human said. I guess he was telling the truth after all."

Pathetic human?

"You tried to make Gary buy you more coins?"

She made no attempt to answer me. "You will order my coins, Watcher."

"It will take five days—"

"Liar. You humans think you're so intelligent, don't you?"

"It will take five days. That's how long it took last time."

She thought on this, perhaps weighing up her options. She didn't have many, she must have realised that. She bent down to stroke Umbra behind the ears.

"Five days," she sneered. "If I do not receive my coins in five days, your human male will die."

"No, no, you can't, it could take longer, it… they could get lost in the post. The seller might post them late. Please… I will need more time." Blind panic consumed me. I remembered the knife in my pocket and reached for it.

A quiet scream travelled from my building to the bridge, taking my attention for a split second. When I turned back, Ivy was gone, and so was that fucking cat.

I stood motionless, unable to register what had happened. All I knew was that I needed to act quickly. I pulled out my phone from my pocket and tried to navigate the auction site, but my hands were shaking. I screamed in frustration and tried again, this time almost dropping my phone. I breathed for five seconds, then out, trying to calm myself. Then I ordered two more coins.

Not knowing what to do, I headed back to my building and saw Sally sitting on the stairs with her head between her knees. The police were frantic on their radios, running up and down the stairs. The fire service was inspecting Gary's door.

"What happened? Where's Gary?" I asked urgently.

"The ambulance took him away... oh Zoe, he was covered in blood. He was down there all this time, alone." She sniffed then sobered. "They did this. They tied him to his chair, tortured him then fled. That's what happened, that's what I will tell the police."

"They?"

"You know who," she snapped at me. "Those scumbags, they did this, then moved out... or... they moved out, then came back... they must have come back tonight. It was them that started the fire, they wanted to cover up their crime."

She stood up abruptly, almost knocking me over, then ran outside to flag down a police officer. I dropped down and sat where she was sitting. Like her, I put my head between my knees. Gary was alive. What had he seen? What would he tell the police? Would he survive the night? I was responsible for this.

"Do you live here?" a police officer asked me.

"I do," I said without looking up.

"Can you answer some questions?"

"I just heard the fire alarm, then knocked on Sally's door," I lied.

"Still, if you could answer a few more questions. It could be helpful."

"Okay."

He asked me if I knew who could have done this and,

thanks to Sally, I had a story. I wouldn't be contradicting her version of events because I needed the time to receive the coins and make the exchange.

"The neighbours who lived opposite Gary, they had started a fire before. I can't think of anyone else it could be," I said mechanically.

I told him that I couldn't stay much longer and that I was going to go and stay with my stepdad. I had nowhere else to go. He accepted this and then I went to find Sally. She was still talking to an officer.

"Sally, I'm going to David's for the night."

"See? See?" She held her hand out for mine, then looked back at the officer. "We're living in terror. We can't even stay in our own homes. I bet they killed that jogger too."

The officer tried to calm her down. "Let's not jump to conclusions."

"Sally," I repeated. "I'm going to David's. You have my number; will you tell me when you know more about Gary?"

"Of course, but you're not walking." She turned from me, then called out to her husband. "Darling? Zoe needs a lift to her stepdad's house, will you do it because I don't think she should be walking there this time of night."

Then, for the officer's ears, she said, "Those people could still be out there."

Her husband nodded his head in agreement, and we walked to the car park behind our flats. In the car we discussed what could have happened. He was with Sally on this; he believed the neighbours did it as well. Not that I could blame them; I'd almost forgotten that they were in the last fire. They must have been frightened. I didn't think about that at the time, and he'd just come back to Sally. Would he leave again? It would be my fault if he did.

When we pulled up to David's, I took a moment to gather myself. "He'll be asleep."

"He'll understand. You go now and my wife will stay in touch. I need to get back to her."

I slipped out of the car. My legs were like jelly when they touched the pavement, then I slowly walked to David's door. I waited for Sally's husband to drive off, but he didn't. He was going to wait until the door was answered. With no choice but to knock, I did it quietly so as not to scare him. Missy started to bark, then after a few seconds, I knocked a little louder.

When David opened the door, Sally's husband drove off.

"Zoe, poppet, what happened?" He ushered me through his door, while rubbing his eyes.

"I spoke with Ivy. I have no choice but to give her the coins," I said, then collapsed to the floor.

***

We stayed up until the early hours, going over and over the night's events. Looking down at my phone made my chest tighten. There were seventeen missed calls from Bowen and four messages. I didn't have the heart to read them. I desperately wanted to switch my phone off, but I wanted to know about Gary as soon as possible.

"What do I do now?" I said, while Missy slept on my lap. David didn't answer. The sun was up now, and I started to wonder where Ivy was now that her hiding place had gone. Oh no, would she hide in my flat? What if Bowen turned up while she was there?

"What's wrong, what are you thinking about?" David asked, as panicked as I felt.

"She could be in my flat now. I will have to tell Bowen where I am."

"Tell him, of course, but don't tell him anything else. At the moment the police will be chasing their own tails. It will give us those five days to think of something."

"We need to think of something other than killing her. She's quick, she won't go down easily." I sighed, knowing that we were going around in circles. I hadn't slept, yet I felt wide awake. I needed to find a way to stop her. I had left my laptop at home, which meant I couldn't do what David wanted me to do: change the story. I had already explained that I had already tried that, but he wanted to see for himself.

"Your diaries. You used to write in diaries when this first started. Here." He stood up and rifled through his cluttered home and found what he was looking for. "A notebook. This could be your diary."

"I've already tried, I can't change them when they're out." I sighed again, with my head in my hands.

I texted Bowen and told him where I was and that I was okay. I needed to avoid him, so I sent another text saying that I still needed space. My heart broke.

"We'll figure it out. We need to act as normal as possible. I'll make us breakfast and take us to work. No, you better call in sick."

"I got sacked yesterday." Strange how I had forgotten that. "Would you mind if I stayed here?"

"Of course. You got sacked?"

I nodded.

"Yes, stay. But you must start a new story. Think of something, a vampire slayer or something." He cringed at his own suggestion.

***

After David left, I tried to sleep. If I could sleep, I could approach this with fresh eyes, maybe even attempt that vampire slayer story. But I was wide awake, buzzing with adrenaline.

I texted Sally a few hours ago and asked how Gary was getting on, but hadn't received a reply yet. Would he live? If he did, would he be complete, body and mind? How could I ever face him again?

A sharp knock on the door startled me. It must be a delivery for David. *More books* I thought.

I decided not to answer it, then I heard Bowen shouting through the letterbox.

"Zoe, I know you're in there. Open up."

His tone was sharp. I stood up, then sat back down. No, I could do this. I wanted to see him as much as I needed to avoid him. I went over to the door and saw through the frosted glass that he was in his uniform.

My phone rang in my hand. It was David.

"Hello." I answered right next to the door. Bowen could both hear and see me at this point. No backing down now.

"Bowen is on his way. He asked me for my address. I didn't know what else to do. Tell him nothing," he ordered.

"He's here, I have to go." I put the phone down and opened the door.

Bowen rushed through and pulled me into him tightly. "I was so worried about you. What's going on? Why haven't you been answering your phone?"

"I just needed time to myself. I'm sorry." I wrapped my arms around him and breathed in his scent. Oh, how I adored this man.

"Sorry for what? Sweetheart, tell me what happened." He ran his hands through my hair.

"I got sacked for cutting a client's ear," I said, trying to keep things off track. I tried to avoid looking at him, but he cupped my face with both his hands and kissed me.

"Let's not worry about that now. What happened last night must have frightened you. Why didn't you ring me? I would have picked you up. You know that." Hot tears streamed down my cheeks while he continued to run his fingers through my hair.

I was at breaking point. Ivy had threatened him, and he needed to prepare himself in case the coins didn't arrive in time. He needed to know, so I kissed him for the last time, committing every second of it to my memory. Then I told him everything.

He laughed at first and tried to convince me that I was tired, wasn't thinking straight. Then he got angry.

"I'm responsible for Amber Morris. Gary almost died," I pleaded with him, trying to make him understand.

"This isn't funny, Zoe, and I don't think you fully understand the seriousness of this." He shook his head. "Are you saying that you tied Gary to that chair?"

He was getting angrier with me now. I had never seen this side to him before.

"No. I could never hurt Gary. Ivy did it."

"Who is Ivy?" he shouted.

"I told you, she's the vampire from my story. She said she would kill you if I didn't get the coins."

"What coins?"

"The coins for the Ferryman."

I had my hand on his arm, but he pulled away and stood up. He started walking around David's living room, knocking books off their piles. He didn't notice.

Then he abruptly stopped and stared down at me.

"You're fucking with me. Is this how you break up with your boyfriends? Fuck with their heads?"

"No. Bowen, please."

His eyes softened. "You're breaking my heart, Zoe. Whatever game you're playing, I want you to stop."

"No, I swear. I'm not fucking with you. I love you, but you have to believe me, please," I begged, but I could already see the outcome. I knew this was coming, but it didn't make it any less painful. I would never forget that look in his eyes.

"Tell me now, right now, that everything you just said is complete crap."

More tears streamed down my cheeks. I felt light-headed, about to pass out. "I can't tell you it's all crap. You saw Umbra yourself, remember?"

"Umbra?"

"The cat."

"Yes, I saw a cat." He rubbed tears from his eyes. "I can't do this right now. I can't. I thought you were different, and you are, but this is too much."

"I'm sorry," I sobbed.

He sniffed, then sobered. "I suggest that you do not talk to my colleagues, you will get charged for wasting police time… or committed."

He turned towards the door and I leapt off the sofa to grab his arm. "Please will you listen?" I begged.

"Off. We're done," he said coldly, then pried my fingers off his arm. He opened the door, took one last look at me, then slammed it shut in my face.

***

Two days had passed since Gary was found, and three days since I last slept. The longest I had ever gone. It was quite amazing really, the things you saw in the corner of your eye, the voices you heard right by your side. The whispering from inside your head. This was what madness felt like, and I allowed it to consume me. Anything was better than the pain I felt. The emptiness.

David wanted me to write. I didn't want to. Writing was the reason I was in this mess. What if I created another character as deadly as Ivy? No, my only option was to kill her.

"I need to go back to mine, see if the coins have been arrived… delivered," I slurred in David's direction.

When he got back from work the day Bowen had left, he knew instantly that I had told him everything. He didn't shout at me or get angry for not listening, he just held me, let me cry until I no longer could. He tried to tell me that everything would be okay. I knew different; nothing would ever be the same again. I was no longer that deer that was staring into the headlights. I was now the deer that was splattered on the side of the road.

"Not like that, you're not. Anyway, I will be going myself, and that's final," he ordered.

"We'll go together in case she's… umm, there."

"Enough of this. You need to sleep. Take the sleeping tablets I got for you, or just lie back and shut your bloody eyes. Sleep."

"Okay. I'll try."

***

My phone rang, waking me up. It was Sally.

"Hello," I croaked, fully clothed on David's sofa.

"Sorry I haven't rung sooner. It's been difficult trying to see Gary and get information out of the doctors. At first, he was unresponsive—"

"Is he okay now?" I was wide awake now.

"Yeah, I think so. The police have been asking him questions all morning."

"They have? What has Gary said?" I felt a glimmer of hope for him, and apprehension for what he would say. Could he even speak?

"I'm not sure, I'm standing in the corridor down from his room, waiting for them to come out."

I smiled at this; it felt foreign, but good. I might not have wanted to be like Sally, but I loved having a person like her in my life. Then, like lightning, panic erupted throughout me. How could I have been so self-absorbed? Careless.

"Sally, where have you been staying? You haven't been back home, have you?" I held my breath, waiting for her to answer.

"No, of course not. Those maniacs could come back, and the police have not said whether they've arrested them or not."

They hadn't been arrested because they were probably lying dead somewhere.

"Good."

"I already knew you were staying away. Your boyfriend has been here, Officer Williams. He's very nice, by the way."

"What else did he say? Is he talking to Gary right now?" I blurted. If Gary told him a vampire attacked him, he might believe me. He needed to stay out of this, but the selfish part of me really wanted him to not think I was completely delusional.

"Just that you're staying at David's. No, he's not talking to Gary, he hasn't been in today. They're coming out. I have to go. Bye, bye, bye."

Sally put the phone down and I was glad. I needed a few minutes of silence.

Gary was alive and Sally was safe.

I was about to ring David when I saw a text from Bowen. I gasped, not quite believing it. My hands shook. My heart couldn't take in any more sorrow; it was filled to the brim. I could just delete it without reading it. Could there be a small chance that he believed me?

> Amber's bite wounds are
> consistent with a dog bite,
> DNA results confirm this.
> Your neighbours have been
> arrested, they were found
> in friend's home.

I screamed, then threw my phone on the floor. What had I done? I went down to my hands and knees and searched for my phone. David's clutter was everywhere. I pushed over pile after pile of books. Finally, I found it. I reread the text over and over, thinking about how to reply. But I had nothing to say. It was over.

CHAPTER 11

Lucy looked worried for me. "So, we discussed last week about how you were under a lot of stress when you believed you were responsible for your neighbours' deaths." She paused. "And then you believed that you were responsible for the jogger's death. Correct?"

"Yeah."

I had to get this off my chest, had to talk about it with someone other than David. Lucy was incredibly understanding last time and really put my mind at ease. Could she do this for a second time? I needed help.

"And then your neighbours again, for a second time."

"Yeah, and that Gary was held captive by Ivy, but if I was wrong about the neighbours and Amber Morris, then perhaps Sally was right about who hurt Gary."

After receiving the text from Bowen, I felt confused, maybe relieved, but only by a little. I shouldn't have said anything to him. If I had waited just a couple more days, I wouldn't have lost him for nothing.

But still, I knew what I saw. I knew I spoke to Ivy. I knew that I kicked Umbra and my foot went straight through her. She even followed me here, which meant I'd only seen her twenty minutes before. I definitely saw her. Or maybe I was seeing things that weren't there, and talking to things that didn't exist. I didn't know what was worse.

A few weeks back, Lucy wanted me to research maladaptive daydreaming. I didn't. I was here to find out what it was, or if I had it.

"I would like to know what changed your mind. What made you believe that you were responsible… again?"

I told her about the conversation I had with David, about how he believed Ivy killed Amber and hid the neighbours' bodies. I went further back, when I first asked him about Umbra, and told Lucy about the mermaids and witches. She looked as confused as I felt.

"It sounds to me that David can be… can be very creative. Perhaps like you, a storyteller," she suggested politely. "Very imaginative, that's the word I was looking for," she quickly added.

"Yeah, we both are, I suppose. We bounce off each other. Are you suggesting that he's put this in my head?" I asked slowly. "That doesn't explain what I saw. I talked to her."

"So, let's talk about what you saw and when. When David suggested that you were responsible, you were again under extreme stress. Yes?" She nodded. Her cue for me to agree.

"Yeah," I nodded back, wanting to get to the point of why I was here. I asked, "Why did you want me to look up maladaptive daydreaming?"

"So, the symptoms are extremely vivid daydreams with your own characters, settings, plots, very detailed story-like features—"

"I do that because I'm thinking about what to write in my head before I type it, that's all," I said defensively.

"Other symptoms include performing repetitive movements while daydreaming, talking out loud, and an overwhelming desire to continue daydreaming. I've seen you do this. You call it spacing out, you're aware of it."

"Talking out loud?" I didn't do that.

"Yeah, I've heard you having a one-sided conversation, while you were sitting opposite me," she said slowly.

That's what I heard behind Gary's door. A one-sided conversation. Oh no, was that me? My skin prickled all over my body. Was I talking to myself and wasn't aware of it? Was it possible that I didn't see Ivy? I did, but she wasn't really there, or just a part of my imagination. Was I even stood on the bridge? Could maladaptive daydreaming really be the cause? I was afraid to ask, but had to.

"What did you hear me say?" My tears started to fall.

Lucy quickly stood to hand me a tissue. "You were playing chess, I believe. You called the person you were playing with 'Father'. I know that you don't refer to anyone in your life as Father. Who was he?"

"That was a scene from my story." That must have been what I heard behind Gary's door, a scene from my story. Why wasn't I aware of it?

"Have I spaced out today, or the last time I saw you?" I quickly asked.

"No, you haven't actually. You do seem to be aware when you do. That's a good thing. Maladaptive daydreaming usually occurs as a coping mechanism in response to trauma, stress, loneliness. Perhaps you use this tool to both escape reality and to write." She smiled in encouragement.

"Could it be possible, not to be aware of it?"

"Not usually. People diagnosed with it are aware of it. Do you feel that you're not always aware when you do it?"

"I'm not sure." I wasn't sure of anything anymore, of what was reality and what was not. My head started to pound.

"Do you know anything about schizophrenia?" she asked in a soft tone.

"I do not have that," I snapped.

"I'm not saying that you do. But some symptoms include hallucinations, hearing and seeing things that don't exist outside of the mind."

Oh shit. Could it be a possibility? I needed to fight against this.

"No. No, I don't have that. You were right, I'm stressed, I don't sleep. I actually just went three days without sleeping and yeah, I did hallucinate, I heard things that weren't there. I was aware of it." I was breathing rapidly now. My heart felt like it was about to explode.

"Calm down, you're okay. Let's start again. You have been under a lot of stress. Your neighbours have gone, been arrested. You are not responsible for any deaths. You can move forward now," she reasoned, standing to hand me another tissue.

"Yeah." What else could I say? I still wasn't entirely convinced.

"Maybe you could keep the creative conversations with David to a minimum. Take some time for yourself. Relax in your own home, sleep regularly."

"I need to do that. I will, then I'll be fine," I said, more to myself than her.

"We're coming to the end of our session. Could you possibly come in twice next week?" she asked casually.

She was worried about me; I could see she was trying to hide it. I hated having to do what I was about to do, but I had no choice.

"I can't come back next week. I lost my job."

***

My walk home seemed to take forever. I was going over everything Lucy had said in my mind, over and over, trying to make sense of it. All I got was a worsening headache. How do I speak to David about this? Was it partly his fault? Lucy seemed to suggest that.

But what would he gain from it? No, he wouldn't hurt me for the sake of it. That being said, perhaps she was right; a break from him wouldn't be a bad thing. At least until this had all blown over.

Every time I felt myself looking out for Umbra, I snapped out of it and focused on my surroundings. I would not give in to this. I would not.

When I rounded the corner towards my home, I saw a white dog sniffing around my building. It looked like Goodboy, except this dog was healthy, and looked strong. Just like how I recreated him. I was still trying to convince myself that he was a different dog, even after I saw my green eyes in his beautiful face. He stopped sniffing and cocked his head as if he sensed me watching.

I will not do this. I will not entertain this. I spun back around and started to walk back the way I came. I'd walk the long way round. I needed to keep my mind off it, so I looked into people's front gardens to get inspiration for our own front garden. It would be nice for when Gary comes home, I thought.

My next attempt to walk back home was successful. No Goodboy. I put my hand on Gary's door and wished him well. I needed to speak to Sally later, see how he was getting on.

As soon as I got in and closed my door, I took Lucy's advice and ran a bath so that I could relax, take twenty minutes to myself. I needed to think about getting a new job, but I'd wait and think about that tomorrow. I also needed to think about my next conversation with David, and what to say to Bowen. Could I make things right with him? I thought not.

My clothes felt baggy on me when I took them off. I needed to eat later. It took me a few seconds to pluck up the courage to look into the mirror. When I finally did, I gave myself a double take. I looked supernatural. My black circles on my white skin looked striking, beguiling. My unkempt long hair looked wild. It suited me.

When I lay back in the bath, the hot water instantly relaxed the tension in my body, but then I remembered the last time I took a bath. I tensed back up. It was with Bowen. We took our time, washing and exploring each other's bodies. I felt brave after having that glass of wine and straddled his lap, making love to him. I couldn't believe I'd lost him. I reached over the bath and grabbed my phone. This would be the last text I sent him. I mentally prepared myself for rejection. It would be okay. I could get through this. I texted him saying sorry, and said that I hadn't slept and that I wasn't thinking straight. I also told him that I had a therapist and that I had been working on myself with her. My heart dropped when I realised, I wouldn't be seeing her again any time soon. I wanted to end the text saying I loved him, then changed my mind. I wouldn't make this harder than it had to be. What I texted was all I could say; that was it.

When I heard a knock at my door, I instantly knew it was Sally. I wasn't getting out of that bath, especially not with tears in my eyes. I rang her instead.

"Hi Sally. I am home. I'm in the bath."

"I thought you were home. Good news, arrests have been made. We'll be staying the night." She sounded tired and not very enthusiastic about the good news.

"How is Gary? Do you know what he said to the police?" I asked this for my own sanity rather than concern. How selfish.

"He didn't say much, I believe. Too traumatised. Which is understandable, can you imagine what he went through?"

"No, I can't." No one could comprehend what he'd been through, even without knowing the full story. Just the way he had been found was horrifying.

"Although he's stable, we won't know when he will be fit enough to leave the hospital. But will he want to come back? I couldn't live in my own home if that happened to me. Could you?"

"No, I couldn't." I wanted to end the call politely. "Can you ring me when you hear anything else?"

"Why don't you ask your boyfriend, he'll know more," she suggested, as hungry for information as I was, although for different reasons.

My heart sank even more when I lied and said, "Yeah, I'll ask him." He hadn't replied to my text yet, and probably wouldn't.

***

After my bath, I lay down on my sofa to text David. How would I word this? I didn't want to upset him, but I had to put myself first. I started by forwarding Bowen's last text. Then I told him that I went to Lucy and texted what she said. I told him that I would be switching my phone off and not to come over, and added that I loved him and not to worry.

Bowen wouldn't be texting back, and Sally could just knock on my door. I switched my phone off and felt somewhat relieved. I felt the quiet that I had longed for, forgetting though, that the quiet came with an emptiness that made you feel numb. Nothing in life is for free, as David always said. I finally understood the meaning of that now.

I flipped the kettle on to make a coffee then decided against it. I needed to sleep soon. I needed to start looking after myself. I went over to my table, fired up my laptop and started to write. In my mind I had called this plesiosaur story Bowen's story, but he would never finish it. My eyes filled with tears again.

I was making good progress when my head started to feel heavy, and I lightly headbutted the keyboard. Without my phone I didn't know what the time was. I stood up on wobbly legs, a pain in my back, and switched the TV on. I scrolled up and down, looking for a news channel. I found one. Two fifteen a.m. Bloody hell.

I sank back into my sofa. Realisation hit me. I didn't need noisy neighbours to keep me up all night; I did this to myself.

I was about to switch it off when I heard the newsreader say, "the aerial video footage shows plesiosaurs in huge numbers swimming along the Isle of Mull coastline. I repeat, plesiosaurs…"

I started to laugh hysterically. I really was losing it. I needed to sleep, but before I did, I had to see this. I shook my head in disbelief. I really shouldn't have entertained this, but at least I was aware that it wasn't real.

The footage was taken earlier today by the looks of it. At first, I thought I saw a pod of whales, then instead of a back flipper breaching the surface, I saw four flippers, two at a time. They rotated them as if they were riding a bike.

This made me smile. They were exactly how I had imagined them in my mind.

I shook my head again then switched it off. I understood what was happening to me now. It was very similar to when I went three nights without sleep. It was a hallucination.

***

Friday morning had been and gone by the time I got up. That was okay though; I had nothing to get up for. I was about to switch on my TV when I remembered what happened last night. What I thought I saw. A niggle in the back of my mind frustrated me. *I will not entertain it*, I chanted. *I will not*. I decided all the same not to switch it on. I wouldn't encourage it.

A sharp, continuous knock rattled my door, pissing me off instantly. Sally did not need to knock on my door like that.

"Zoe. Open up."

Is that... no, it couldn't be. I looked through my spyhole.

"Open up, now. We know you're in," Bowen shouted from behind my door.

What did he want? Was he angry about how we left things? Was it about the text I sent him yesterday? I didn't think I could handle his anger towards me. I decided not to answer the door.

"Poppet, let us in." David's voice sounded urgent.

He came into view of my spyhole. What was he doing here, with Bowen? Oh shit. Did they think I was at risk of hurting myself? Well, I wasn't. That thought never crossed my mind. I wanted to fight back the madness, and I was.

I heard Sally open up her door and ask them what was going on.

"We're just here to see if she's alright," Bowen said casually.

"She's fine. I spoke to her yesterday. Can you believe the news? I think it's a prank, don't you?" she said excitedly. "I have her spare key in case of an emergency. Shall I get it?"

"No," I shouted, then opened my door. "I'm fine."

They both rushed through, almost knocking me over. Bowen wrapped his arms around me, kissed my temple then ran past me into my living room. David turned back to close the door on Sally.

"Where is it? There it is," Bowen said urgently. He went straight to my table and opened up my laptop.

"Where's the controller for the TV?" David said, frantically searching for it. "I got it."

I calmly sat on my sofa, wondering if this was a hallucination too. Why were they acting like this? Not knowing what to do, I went to my bathroom to brush my teeth. Maybe when I came back out, they'd be gone. I walked back into my living room to make the most of Bowen. I missed him so much already. Would he fade away before my eyes?

"Zoe. What are you doing?" David looked bemused.

"'Rushing, ma, 'eeth," I said, then stepped back into my bathroom to spit the toothpaste down my sink. There was blood in the foam. I needed to floss more. "What are you doing here?"

He followed me into the bathroom. "Haven't you seen the news?"

"No. Not this morning, I haven't."

"It's here. Isle of Mull." Bowen called out from my living room. "That's what she wrote."

"I told you," David called back.

I walked through my living room to my kitchen and flipped on the kettle. "Do you both want a coffee?"

"No, we do not want a coffee," David snapped. "What's wrong with you?"

Nothing's wrong with me, I wanted to say, but I couldn't. Everything felt so surreal, like a vivid dream perhaps. When I looked over at Bowen, unfallen tears filled my eyes. When I tried to tell him what I thought was the truth a couple of days ago, he looked scared for me, but now he looked scared of me. I went over to put my arms around him. He stepped back.

"What are you?" he asked slowly.

"I'm nothing, I mean, I'm normal. I'm sorry I said all that crap the other day. I was tired, wasn't thinking straight. I'm okay now," I cried. *Please give me another chance,* I mentally begged.

David came over and cupped my face. "I told him everything, poppet. He came to mine this morning, looking for you—"

"Told him what?" I looked over at Bowen. "It's not true, whatever he told you. It's not true."

Bowen pointed to my TV. "That's your story. You tried to tell me. I didn't believe… still can't." He went down on to one knee, then the other.

I went over to him and ran my fingers through his hair, then looked over at the TV. I didn't want to accept it, but if he could see them too… he was here, wasn't he? This was real? If not, I would go back to Lucy and get further help.

I looked at David. He nodded his head in encouragement. "I know it's scary Zoe, but you know the truth. Don't hide from it. Ivy will be coming back soon."

"Ivy won't—"

145

"Gary said he let a woman into his home, at first he thought it was you," Bowen said quietly. He frowned, then shook his head. "He said that she threatened him, tried to make him buy coins, coins for the Ferryman… umm… and that she drank from him, like a vampire."

I continued to stroke his hair, then ran my hands down his back. So, someone else other than me had seen her. I looked back at my TV and watched my beautiful plesiosaurs pedalling just under the surface of the ocean.

"His injuries are consistent with bite er… er, umm, loss of blood also." He sounded like he was going into shock. "My colleagues believe a weapon was used, but… he said, Ferryman."

"I'm sorry, Bowen," I said, putting my head to his.

"Poppet." David knelt beside us. "She will be coming back. Have the coins arrived?"

"No, they haven't. Should be here by tomorrow."

I once again felt fear run through my veins. I didn't know why she didn't kill my neighbours. Maybe they had fled that night, and I didn't know why she hadn't killed Gary. Maybe she left him alive, hoping he'd eventually get her the coins. Why didn't he get her the coins? I knew though that she was a killer, and she had threatened Bowen. She needed to be stopped.

But I still couldn't shake off that last bit of doubt. That annoying niggle in the back of my mind had switched sides, and was now batting for the other team. This could still be a delusion. I needed more proof. The TV in front of me or what Bowen had said wasn't enough.

I leapt up and ran out of my door and almost fell down my stairs, taking two at a time. I heard David and Bowen calling after me.

I was shouting out before I had even left the building.

"GOODBOY, GOODBOY. Where are you, boy? GOODBOY."

I spun around and around, looking for him. David and Bowen were behind me.

"Is that him?" Bowen said, looking towards the bridge. "It can't be."

Goodboy frantically wagged his tail, and jumped up and down on his front paws. I ran towards him and he towards me. I braced myself for his weight, but instead he ran right through me. It felt like pins and needles. We both turned around together and tried again, this time slower. My hand passed through him. I tried again. He whined, desperate for my touch.

"Good dog, Goodboy. I've missed you, I have," I sang, in my soppy doggy voice. "I've missed you."

My hand made contact, on and off. His unblemished white coat felt like silk and shone silver in the light. "You're new to this, Goodboy. Takes practice." Well, that was my guess, anyway. The calmer he became, the more I could stroke him.

I looked over his head and saw that David and Bowen were still standing down the bridge. Bowen looked bewildered. It was one thing believing what others had said, or seeing something on the TV. But seeing one of my creations up close must have been frightening, disorientating.

David looked almost satisfied. He too must have felt like he was losing his marbles at some point throughout this. He might have seen my characters from my little stories when I was younger, but not my recent ones. Not even Umbra had shown her face to him since I was a child, and yet he still believed me.

When I walked towards them, Goodboy followed, wagging his tail.

"He has your eyes," Bowen said, unbelieving. He stepped forward to stroke him, then changed his mind. Goodboy seemed to recognise him and made an attempt to nuzzle him. His muzzle went through Bowen's hand, and he shivered.

"I don't know if I'm ready for this," Bowen whispered to himself.

"You don't have to be. You don't need to have any part of this," I assured him.

"I've heard about people who can read minds, move objects… not that I believe any of that, but… Zoe, what are you?" He came over to me and put his hands on my shoulders and looked into my eyes.

He was searching for something, perhaps the truth. What was the truth? It was time to accept myself for what I was, and what I could do.

"What are you?" he repeated.

"I am the Watcher."

CHAPTER 12

Goodboy sniffed every piece of furniture, every inch of my floor and every object in my home. He looked so happy, apart from when he walked past his old home on the way to mine. His heckles rose, and he growled in a way that promised death. He remembered his past because I didn't think to erase it, but I was glad now that I hadn't. I was glad that he remembered me. I needed him as proof of my sanity.

Out of curiosity I filled up a bowl of water to see what he would do. He sniffed it once, went back for another sniff, then walked off. He would never starve again, never go thirsty. He was immortal now. Safe.

I went into my room and balled up a pair of socks to throw for him. He tilted his head curiously. Of course, he didn't know how to play. No one had ever played with him. Varik fed him, before I changed him. He walked him, took care of him, but never thought to play with him.

"I think he's just enjoying our company, poppet." David smiled towards Goodboy. "Who's a special boy, who's a special doggy? You are," he sang, then stroked Goodboy's back. He was becoming more tangible now.

Goodboy play-bowed to David, tail high in the air, wagging. My heart was lifted. I might have created monsters, but I had also created something special, something beautiful. The news was still on. It had been running non-stop. All other programmes had been cancelled for the day. My plesiosaurs were also special like Goodboy. But they would need help. Already, the camera crews on boats and from helicopters had been getting too close, frightening them. They would be hunted too; I had no doubt.

Bowen couldn't decide what to look at; his gaze flickered from Goodboy to the news.

"When will whalers start hunting them?" he asked, reading my mind.

"I'm not sure. Soon. It's what would happen though, Bowen, in reality. Even if this wasn't part of my story, that would happen." My heart broke for him. He had been so upset when he read that part. They were after all his favourite dinosaurs. Even if they weren't, it would be a tragedy to watch them disappear.

"One thing at a time," David interjected. "We need to discuss Ivy."

"You're right, but I still don't know what to do when she'll show. If the coins don't arrive today or tomorrow…" I was unable to finish my sentence, unable to think about Bowen being hurt, or worse.

"What were her words Zoe, exactly?" Bowen asked.

"'Coins, or your human male dies'. She referred to you as my male."

"Could I fight her off, knife her in the heart?" He laughed without humour. "This is ridiculous, I can't… I can't go there."

"And you won't have to, I promise. I will end her when the time comes."

"How? And why can't you put her back in the story?"

"Even if I could, I wouldn't know the exact time she enters the gateway."

"What gateway?" He shook his head. David said that he'd told him everything, and I thought I had. A lot of small details had been left unsaid.

I offered to start again from the very beginning, from how the vampires got trapped in the first place, to the Hellfire Caves and the many other gateways that they housed.

"Why don't you write about how she travelled back, through the gateway, then close it, or have it so that it never existed?" Bowen offered.

It pleased me that he now believed me, and he deserved to know the truth. But he couldn't be a part of this.

"Because it wouldn't make sense. David, you were right. In order for the characters to become…" I looked over at Goodboy, and an idea came to me.

"I changed Goodboy halfway through the story. At first, I just gave him a loving home, one where he was just a dog, then I made it so that he couldn't starve again. He became a phantom, like Umbra."

"The second version was more accurate, because he died in real life. You know you can't change her once she's out," David said.

"How about the witches in the woods? You said that I wrote a story about how they travelled to New Orleans."

"You gave them a dream of a free and happy life. With Ivy, you gave her a mission, a purpose. She needs to free her people, her father." He frowned as if trying to solve a puzzle. "Your characters will and can fight against you, depending on how defiant you made them."

And a queen would be defiant.

"How about I change the Inner Temple? I already have. I could flood the realm with demons. She would be captured, killed."

"Then the demons would get hold of the coins."

"Oh yeah, er, plus Varik is still there. I don't want him harmed." Goodboy whined and wagged his tail frantically at the mention of his name. He bounced around then headed towards my door, jumping straight through it.

"Where's he gone?" Bowen asked, standing up. He shook his head, unable to believe what he saw.

"My guess is that he went back to Varik. I know this sounds strange because Goodboy died only a few weeks ago, but Varik has taken care of him for almost three decades... I think." Heat crept over my face. I wasn't entirely sure when they got together because I didn't give them a backstory, I just knew that they'd been trapped in the Inner Temple for twenty-eight years.

"Who's Varik?"

"Another vampire. If Ivy went back, she would recognise Varik, but he wouldn't know who she was. I made him and Goodboy the sole survivors."

"What would happen if she did go back?" Bowen asked.

"Her home as she knows it is gone. She will come straight back out."

"We need to kill her," David said. "We need to discuss how we're going to do that, and not worry about how to get her back in the story. How many coins did you order?"

"I was panicking when I ordered them. I only ordered two."

"Did she want a specific amount?"

"No, she didn't say."

"We could fill up a bag of ones and twos, throw them on the floor, then when she bends down to pick them up, chop off her head."

I smiled at David, and he returned it with a frown. "What?"

"You haven't met her. If you throw the coins on the floor, she will order you to pick them up."

We both gave up and looked over at Bowen. I thought he was watching the news. He wasn't. He was staring at us like we were aliens. I couldn't help feeling extreme guilt for dragging him into this; he didn't deserve it. Had I messed him up? Would he go through what I had been through in the last couple of weeks, thinking himself mad? I didn't know how to put this right.

"Are you okay?" I asked him slowly.

He nodded his head yes, then walked over to the kitchen. "Coffee?"

He's snapped, I thought. "Yeah, thank you." I went over to help him, and he wrapped his arms around me. He held me for so long I didn't think he'd let go.

"Poppet," David said to get our attention. "I'm going to head back. We have one more night before she shows. I need to find something strong enough and big enough to take her head off. Zoe, switch your phone back on. I will be back tomorrow morning."

I walked over to hug him goodbye. I couldn't believe I ever thought I needed distance from this man. How thoughtless of me. I told myself that I hadn't been thinking straight, and I hadn't, but I should never have doubted David.

"When the time comes, you need to keep Bowen away," he whispered in my ear.

I nodded yes.

***

In the evening, Bowen phoned his colleagues and called in sick. He was planning on helping me and David. I needed to convince him otherwise.

He hadn't said much since David left. He just sat and stared in the direction of the TV, but I knew he wasn't really watching it. He wore a permanent frown on his face. My guess was that he was trying to make sense of today's events, and to make sense of me.

"I'm sorry I didn't believe you," he finally said.

"Sorry? You have nothing to be sorry about, this is my mess, but I promise you, had I known all of this for certain, I never would have dragged you into it." I looked down to the floor. "I wouldn't have agreed to go out with you."

He sat closer to me so that he could stroke my hair from my face. He leant forward and lightly kissed me.

"I wouldn't have gotten to know you if you'd said no. I'll admit, being a police officer, I thought I'd seen it all, or I'd be better prepared to accept…" He spun his finger in the air, as if trying to find the words. He eventually gave up. "My point is, I should have listened."

"Come on, no one would have believed me. I didn't believe me. I woke up this morning thinking that I was crazy. When you and David came in, I wasn't even sure if it was real." I smiled at him, wanting him to feel better.

"Okay, but I still feel shitty about it." He smiled back. "Anyway, what's a Watcher, why are you a Watcher?"

"My characters from the Inner Temple named me the Watcher. They could feel me watching them. They were right; I was, in a way. I was watching their story unfold while I wrote it."

"They called you the Watcher?" His eyes were softening; he was trying to understand it.

There was one question on my mind. I didn't want to bring it up, but I had to know. "What happened with Amber Morris? One minute it couldn't have been a dog, the next it was."

"The attack seemed too savage. Her head was almost detached from her body." He looked sick. There was no way he could be a part of David's and my non-existent plan to take down Ivy. There was only one way to kill her.

He kissed my forehead. "I heard what David said, about keeping me away. Zoe, I will not leave you to fight that, that thing. We will do this together."

"I don't want you to get hurt. I couldn't live with it." I felt desperate to make him understand. "Please stay out of this, Bowen."

"And I couldn't live with it if you got hurt. I can't walk away now, not knowing what I know now. I'm helping."

We sat close with our hands on each other, my hand on his jaw and his massaging the back of my neck. I realised then that I couldn't keep him away, even if I wanted to; he knew too much. The selfish part of me was glad that he wanted to stay.

"When this is over, are we still over?" It was a childish question considering what was at stake, but I needed him tonight; needed to be close to him.

"No, we're not over. But from now on, you tell me everything, and that includes all the small details. Okay?"

"Okay." I ran my hand down his chest. "Will you stay tonight?"

"I was planning on it." He grinned.

We kissed deeply, and all my worries evaporated. He pulled my jumper over my head, and I straddled his lap.

Then, arching my back, needing to be closer to him, he trailed his mouth from my neck to my breasts. I loved it when he did that. We were both breathing heavily, desperate for each other.

"Here or in the bedroom?" he whispered, standing up with my legs still wrapped around his waist.

"Here."

***

"Are you certain you want to be a part of this?" David asked. "I hope you realise what you're dealing with. She's not some drunk who's smashed a window or robbed a packet of Twiglets from the supermarket, she's a vampire."

"I know that," Bowen snapped.

They had been arguing in my living room for about twenty minutes. I listened to them from my bedroom while I was still in bed. Bowen was adamant he was coming, and David didn't like it.

"So, what's your plan then, handcuff her? Think about your career, your life. It will all go away if you start talking."

"I'm not talking about this to anyone," he snapped again, then smugly said, "and what is your plan? That thing by the door."

I wasn't sure what that thing was, by the door, but Bowen didn't sound impressed. Since David and I hadn't come up with a plan yet, it was worth hearing him out.

"We don't have many options, do we?"

"I can use my taser. Zoe said Ivy knows very little about technology."

"Okay good. You taser her, then I'll use that."

"Look at the size of it, she'll see it."

My door buzzer went off. Bowen answered. "Yeah, come up mate."

I quickly jumped out of bed, shoved my legs into a pair of joggers, and pulled up a jumper off the floor. Who was that? Please tell me they haven't got someone else involved in this. Bowen just said he wouldn't be talking to anyone. I was about to open my bedroom door when I heard my front door being opened.

"Can you sign for me here?"

Ah, it's the coins. My heart dropped. I went back into my room and sat on my bed, head in my hands. Tonight, I would meet with Ivy.

***

All three of us were standing on the bridge. Umbra hadn't shown her rotten face, not that I knew of, so it was the only place I could think of to meet her. We had discussed whether or not to take the coins; the last thing we wanted was for her to go back, but if we didn't have the coins, what would she do to Bowen? I already knew and couldn't risk him. We needed a plan B, but it was just as bad as the first.

That thing by the door that Bowen wasn't impressed with was an axe, but what else could we use? He was right about one thing. Ivy would see it and know what we were planning. David had no choice but to hold it by his side.

"What if she doesn't show?" Bowen asked.

"I don't know," I answered honestly.

"She'll show," David said, trying to keep the axe close to his leg.

My adrenaline spiked at David's words. The new plan was for me to hand her the coins, then for Bowen to use his taser, then for David to use the axe. In that order. Afterwards, we were going to put her body under the bridge. Would it smell, decompose like a human body? I didn't know, but something told me it wouldn't.

We stood facing each other, faces expressionless. I started to feel agitated. Had she already found the coins through a different source? Where had she been hiding all this time? I looked over at the moon above my building. It gave me the peace that I needed to calm my nerves.

Something out of place caught my eye, something I should have noticed before, but I hadn't thought to look up.

"She's standing on my roof," I said calmly, and I did feel calm. Why?

They both spun around to look up. Ivy lifted her hand, pointed her finger up, then wagged it at us, as if we were naughty children. She then turned to walk off the roof, towards the back of the building. We were back to not knowing her location. She could come from any direction.

"That was her," Bowen said.

"Yeah, get ready. She's coming."

We all turned around, looking left to right. "Stand back to back," Bowen ordered. We did.

Her laugh echoed from under the bridge. It sounded like mine. Bowen looked in my direction to confirm it wasn't me.

We heard a splash in the water below, then a thump on the bridge wall to our right. It was her. Her wide smile showed off her teeth. Both Bowen and David jumped back. Her smile widened even more. She was amused.

"Watcher? You brought your male with you. This surprises me." She looked anything but surprised.

"Stay away from her," Bowen said, standing in front of me.

I needed to be able to see her, and I didn't want Bowen to get hurt. I kept my hand on his back and stepped to the side of him.

"I have your coins," I said. The confidence in my voice was no way a reflection of how I felt.

"Your male means much to you." She sniffed at the air in David's direction. "The other one is not your male, nor your father."

"I'm her stepfather," he said. Why did he tell her that?

She sneered at him, looked down on him like shit on her shoe. She did not approve of him speaking without being spoken to first.

"My coins, Watcher," she demanded, standing motionless.

While reaching into my back pocket, I noticed both David and Bowen tense up. If I had noticed it, so would she. I could already see the outcome.

I kept my hand in my pocket, coins in hand. She cocked her head, calculating my next move, then looked at David's axe, then at the mysterious object in Bowen's hand.

She grinned then rushed forward, faster than any speed I had encountered before. She knocked both Bowen and David off their feet to the floor. She pushed me back, using both her hands on my shoulders. My feet left the ground. I tensed, waiting for the impact. It never came. She was behind me now, holding me up, trying to wrench my hand from my pocket. Her hands felt like ice on my skin. I screamed as her claws raked my palm as she took the coins. My heart pounded in my cars and I fell to the floor. When I looked up, she was standing back on the bridge wall.

"Watcher, I will be back," she promised, then jumped into the water. This time there was no splash.

Bowen scrambled towards me. "Are you okay? Let me see." He ran his hands over my body, looking for injuries.

I lifted my palm up. It was filled with blood that vibrated in my shaking hand.

"Are you okay?" My voice trembled. "David? Are you okay?"

He was looking over the bridge, but he wouldn't find her. She was long gone. She knew what we had planned. Why didn't she kill them? Because she wanted more coins. She would be back, as promised.

"Nothing a strong whisky won't cure." His tone betrayed his bravado. He knelt beside me. "Poppet, we will take you to the hospital."

Bowen nodded in agreement.

"No. It looks worse than it is," I lied. My hand was burning.

We all stood up. My legs felt weak. As we headed to my building, our heads flickered all around, looking out for her.

"How long do you think we have before she comes back?" Bowen asked.

Neither of us answered.

CHAPTER 13

A few weeks had passed since that night. We didn't say much when we got back to my flat. What was there to say? Our plan was useless, and we didn't have a back-up one. I tried in vain to write about Ivy's return to the Inner Temple, but it all fell flat. I couldn't think about what Varik would say to her, couldn't even give him a reason to kill her. Bowen and David kept trying to persuade me to close the gateway. But I couldn't destroy the gateway, even if I wanted to; there was no description of how it existed in the first place.

For the first three days, David stayed at mine. He did want us to stay at his, but I worried about Sally, didn't want Ivy coming back without me being there, and I didn't want Ivy to use my home as a new hiding place.

We all drove back to his home to pick up Missy and some clothes. He also put a sign on his shop door saying he'd be closed due to illness. Missy was a good distraction to have. She didn't have a care in the world and that somewhat brought us a sliver of normality, even when Goodboy came and went. It was interesting watching him and Missy interact.

The news was also a distraction; it no longer broadcast just my plesiosaurs swimming in their new natural habitat. It now showed interviews from scientists, palaeontologists and ecologists. Apparently, the plesiosaurs had been discovered now due to climate change. Something to do with the ocean's temperature rapidly changing. Some believed they had simply gone unnoticed and reminded the viewers that we knew more about space than we did our ocean.

Either way, it had changed the world. People were acting as if an alien aircraft had landed in their back garden. There were protests throughout London. People were demanding to know the truth, and wanted to know if the plesiosaurs were real, or fake news. Some were accusing the government of covering up a science experiment gone wrong. That amused me. Others had cottoned on quickly and protested with anti-hunt signs. This gave me hope.

We couldn't stay holed up in my flat for much longer, we all knew that. David suggested we go back to work, and I was to come with him. Bowen was pleased by that, not wanting me to be left there by myself, and he couldn't keep taking time off sick. Three days was enough. We couldn't have his colleagues asking questions or questioning his work ethic.

"I can't offer you much money, it might be below minimum wage," David had said the first morning we opened.

"I don't expect money," I argued.

"You can't work here for free, and if I'm honest I was going to offer you a job anyway. I can't keep doing it six days a week."

"Okay," I had said.

The day had been slow, but stress free. I hadn't realised how demanding working with the general public was until I started here. I mean yeah, we still had customers asking us for specific books and recommendations, but it was so different to the never-ending conveyor belt of client after client sitting in your chair every twenty minutes. I felt like I could breathe, like I was free.

But I had loved barbering, hadn't I? Maybe. I just kind of fell into it, I suppose. I needed pocket money when I was a kid, to buy what I wanted, and not just stuff for school. So, I got a job sweeping hair for this old-fashioned barber shop when I was thirteen. The owner, Richard, suggested I start an apprenticeship, and I couldn't think of anything else I wanted to do when I left school, so I agreed.

"David, I'm going to run over to the post office to post these books."

He shook his head at me from behind his desk.

With Bowen's help I created an online shop for David, selling his second-hand books. I spent my days taking photos of books, front, back and spine. Then uploaded the images with the price and offer of free postage. We may have been quiet today, but we'd made just as much money, if not more. Plus, the shop was starting to look tidy.

"My shop's starting to look empty," he said dryly.

I rolled my eyes at him. "This is what selling your stock looks like. Anyway, it makes room for new books."

"I don't sell new books."

"You know what I mean," I laughed, and it felt good.

Although I still had the threat of Ivy returning, I somehow felt relaxed, and even though my eyes were still ringed with black circles, I slept. Maybe it had something to do with Bowen moving in, I didn't know, but I hadn't slept this well and so deeply in years. I felt focused.

After returning from the post office, I helped David close the shop down. We walked back to the car and talked about everything and nothing. This too felt good.

"I do appreciate what you're doing, poppet," he said, then smiled before opening his car door and lifting Missy in.

I got in then closed the door. "Are you sure? I know you don't like to see your books walking out the door, but we can start going to book fairs again," I offered.

"Yeah, we can, I'd like that." He put both his hands on the steering wheel and sighed.

"What is it?" But I already knew. I wanted to convince myself it was just about the books, but couldn't. We couldn't keep avoiding it.

"She could come back at any time. I worry about it."

"So do I, but you said we needed to live our lives as normal as possible."

"We do, we should. But the worry of it keeps me awake." He looked over at me, and for the first time I noticed how tired he looked. Guilt consumed me.

"I'm sorry David, I don't know what to say, or what to do when she comes back. I try not to think about it."

"I know you do. Look, I have something for you, and I don't want you to argue with me about it." He reached over me and opened the glove compartment.

He handed me a white envelope.

"What's this?" I frowned.

"It's my will."

I tried to shove the envelope back into his hand. "David, no."

"Listen, I'm sixty-two next week. I have to start thinking about things like this. If it helps, I had it drawn up years ago, but I'm giving it to you now."

"Why now?" I cried. The thought of him dying made my heart drop. He was the only family I had.

"Well, it did take me a few weeks to find it, if I'm honest," he grinned, trying to make light of it. "I've left everything to you, including Missy, of course."

"I can't think about this right now." I wouldn't.

"I know, and you don't have to. Just take it home with you, keep it safe. Let me sleep well tonight knowing that I've done everything I can. Okay?"

"Okay," I said quietly, rubbing my tears away.

"Is Bowen home or are you coming to mine?"

"Bowen's home," I answered, unable to look at him.

"Come on then, let's get going."

***

Bowen was in the kitchen when I walked through the door. I kicked my shoes off and hung up my coat.

"Hey sweetheart. I'm making a mushroom pasta bake, if that's okay with you." He turned from the sink. "What's wrong?"

My eyes were probably still red from crying in David's car. I couldn't talk about the envelope he gave me. I needed to put that to the back of my mind. "We were discussing Ivy," I said. Not a complete lie.

Bowen, like me, had also put it to the back of his mind. He held out his arms for me to walk into.

"I know it's hard, but we don't know if she will come back. We can't live our lives constantly looking over our shoulders." He kissed me, then went back to the kitchen.

"Goodboy has been here today looking for you," he said, trying to cheer me up.

I smiled at the mention of his name. He had been coming and going every day, splitting his time between us, and I assumed, Varik. At first Bowen was sceptical, but Goodboy soon won him over.

"I'm getting used to him. I got him that ball over there," he said, pointing to it on the table. "He doesn't bring it back, but he does like chasing it."

I smiled again. He was right, we couldn't keep looking over our shoulders. I looked down at my clawed palm, almost healed.

***

Bowen's phone rang, making both of us jump awake. What time was it? He must be getting called in early.

"Is that your work?" I croaked.

"It's your phone," he mumbled.

The phone's light flashed underneath my PJs on the floor.

"It's David." Panic erupted throughout me. Oh no.

I was afraid to answer, so Bowen took the phone off me. "David? Hello?"

Maybe David dialled by accident.

I took the phone back. "Hello."

"Watcher?"

I stood up fast, not really knowing what else to do. What did I need to do? What could I do? My worst nightmare was happening to me right now. A nightmare that I'd buried so deep, it couldn't surface without my permission.

Tears streamed down my face as I heard David calling out, "I love you poppet, don't come over. Stay where you are."

Missy was barking aggressively in the background.

"You killed my father," Ivy screeched. "Now yours must die."

"*No. No,*" I screamed down the phone.

I heard David begging for his life. He was crying.

Snap.

Either David or the phone had dropped to the floor. I was screaming. I couldn't stop screaming and shaking. I couldn't focus while I relayed what I'd just heard. I felt sick. Bowen took the phone from me.

"David. David," he shouted down the phone.

He raced around to his side of the bed and called the police. His voice was frantic, panicked. He repeated David's address a couple of times.

I didn't hear what else he said. Something about a break. in. It didn't matter. I needed to get to David's house. He'd need help. He'd been bitten, like Gary, and he'd need to go to the hospital. Maybe he'd need a blood transfusion. He'd be alright.

***

I was sitting on David's sofa, and my temporary bed, while the funeral director zipped up the body bag. The police and medical services confirmed it was an accidental death before having his body removed.

He'd tripped over his hoarded belongings and broke his neck while on the phone to me, it had been decided by the police, although I believed Bowen may have influenced that decision. They didn't question why he was ringing me at three in the morning, or maybe they did. I couldn't recall. They tried to ask me questions, but I couldn't hear them, and even if I could, I couldn't answer. Words would not come, even when they stood on David's books and chess pieces. I wanted to scream at them to stop, but nothing came out.

Bowen tried to comfort me by holding me close, but I couldn't feel him. My body was numb.

Then the funeral director tried to give me his card, but my arms wouldn't cooperate. So, he left it on David's glass coffee table, while Bowen shook hands with his colleagues at the door. I thought Officer Blake was with them, thought I recognised his voice. Not that it mattered.

Missy whined by my feet. Finally, my arms woke up. I picked her up so I could comfort her. She nestled in my lap. I couldn't imagine the horrors she must have seen. She must have been so frightened. It was then that I smelt her urine among David's hoarded treasures. Poor girl. I'd never forget seeing her lying on David's body when we first arrived. It was through the window because Bowen wouldn't let me enter. He did say why but I couldn't recall.

Bowen turned my face to his. "Zoe?"

"You're next," I said out loud, not thinking before speaking.

"Hey, what was that sweetheart?" he said, while stroking my hair from my face. He sat closer to me, as close as he could get.

"She'll come after you next. I didn't just take her father away; I took her whole world away." And she would stop at nothing until she took mine.

"I won't let that happen," he vowed.

"We need to find her."

We should have been looking for her this whole time instead of agonising over the possibility of her return. We'd pushed it to the back of our minds and tried to move on. We all did, or so I thought up until yesterday. David hadn't moved on; he'd tried to tell me, but I wouldn't listen. I didn't want to. If I had, I might have remembered Ivy's greatest weakness.

"She's blind in the sun," I whispered.

***

Bowen was helping me pack Missy's food and toys into a box. "It's for the best that his death is registered as an accident. I hope you agree." He ran his hand down my back.

I nodded.

"I think this is what David would have wanted. He would have done the same."

He was right. David didn't want us talking to the police. He said we'd be laughed at. Poor Gary had been laughed at. Bowen told me that even though Gary was adamant he'd been bitten and drunk from, the police were still searching for a weapon. There weren't many animals out there with a double row of teeth, and none that could explain the blood loss.

I nodded again and wondered how Bowen was holding up, having had to lie to his colleagues. Was he feeling conflicted? Would he regret being in my life? Would I lose him again?

"Come on, sweetheart, let's get back. I've taken the week off to be with you. We can come back, do a little bit at a time."

***

Once home, Bowen guided me to the bedroom to help me get undressed. I was still wearing PJs. It was all I could find when I dressed in a panic.

"I'll run you a bath, okay?"

"Thank you," I said, before I heard my letterbox squeaking open.

"Zoe, it's Sally," she called through.

"Could you talk to her? Please. Tell her what happened," I sobbed. I wasn't ready to talk, would probably never be. I also wanted a minute to myself; there was something I needed to do.

"Yeah, of course," he said, kissing my hand before answering the door.

My phone was somewhere in this room. I had thrown it somewhere, looking for something to wear. Sally would be keeping Bowen busy, so I had time. I looked under my bed. Found it.

This felt different to the last two times I visited this auction site. The first time was out of curiosity and wishful thinking. The second time was out of desperation. This time it was for revenge. I clicked pay now.

***

In the five days I had to wait for the coins, Bowen and I went to David's and moved a few boxes of books at a time to his bookshop. He told me he and Sally would be arranging the funeral and for me not to worry about a thing. What would I have done without him? I couldn't comprehend how much I loved him sometimes. I certainly didn't deserve him. Sally too had been amazing, bringing hot dinners for us and asking if I needed anything. She also offered to help clear David's belongings, but I wasn't ready for anyone to touch his stuff.

Bowen asked me one morning if I had contacted my mum.

"Yeah, I already have. No reply," I said. No reply. No surprise.

I decided to block her number. It was time to move on. It felt right.

We also walked Missy every morning and every afternoon. This was my new routine; I needed one. Goodboy came with us too. We would stand by the door and Bowen would call out his name, and after a few seconds he would appear.

I tried to tell Bowen about the strange looks he got, when he threw the ball and then chased after it in the opposite direction to the only dog that people could see. He just grinned and shrugged his shoulders. "Oh, well. If he's happy, I'm happy."

I was happy that they were getting on, but I had long suspected something, something that might make Bowen think twice about Goodboy, but I had to ask. I couldn't keep putting things in the back of my mind. I wouldn't do that anymore. I had to take responsibility.

I looked down at Goodboy. "Do you think it was him that killed Amber Morris?"

Bowen nodded yes, surprising me. He had never hinted at the possibility.

"Then it was my fault," I said quietly, unable to look at him.

He threw the ball to Goodboy, then held me to his chest. "No, it's not your fault. If he hadn't been abused, you wouldn't have brought him back. That's the way I see it, and that's how I want you to see it. Okay?"

But I couldn't. If it wasn't for my story, both Amber and David would be alive.

Gary had also come home. Both he and Sally came to my door to offer their condolences. Gary was wearing a high turtleneck jumper and looked like a ghost of the man he once was. When he held out a bunch of flowers to me, he flinched back when I stepped forward to thank him. He was scared of me; to him I looked too similar to Ivy. It was, after all, why he let her in. My voice probably haunted him too, so I just nodded and quietly mumbled.

Sally warned me before he came to my door that he didn't want to talk about what happened to him while he was being held captive. I couldn't blame him. Sally told the police it was the neighbours who did this to him. I believe in the end Gary just went along with it. All he said was that it could have been a possibility. His statement led to the arrest of the neighbours. They were now being held in remand because they no longer had a fixed address. Not that I gave a shit. They were getting what they deserved. However, when the time was right, I would sit down with Gary and tell him the truth, from start to finish. He deserved to know, and he would be able to do whatever he wanted with that truth.

When the coins finally arrived, I had to lie to Bowen. It killed me to do so, but I had no choice.

"What's that, sweetheart?"

"Oh, just women's things," I said mechanically.

He was too distracted to detect my lie. There was a vampire on the loose. A vampire that was still a threat to us, and he was on high alert. He also wasn't sleeping. This broke my heart.

Why Ivy hadn't come back yet I didn't know. She would get hungry soon; she'd need to feed. Who would be her next meal? I wondered why she hadn't fed from David, glad she hadn't. The thought of it made me retch. But I knew why she hadn't. To her, her father had just died. When David went, I couldn't eat either.

Bowen was going back to work in two days. Luckily for me it was a night shift, and I needed the night to myself.

From now until then I would not sleep.

I needed my mind to be on the brink of madness.

CHAPTER 14

"Okay, I have to go now, I will be back no later than six, maybe six fifteen," Bowen said, as he laced up his shoes. "If you need me for anything, no matter how small—"

"I'll be fine, I promise." I smiled, trying to assure him.

He straightened up. "If you feel scared or you see something out of the ordinary—"

I pulled his head down and kissed him. "I'll be fine. You have done so much for me already. You need to get back to normality."

"Normality. What's that?" He smiled, his beautiful brown eyes softening. "I wouldn't change a thing, just so you know. Not one thing."

"I love you."

"I love you too. Please try and get some sleep if you can."

***

As soon as the door closed, I walked over to my table and fired up my laptop. My hands shook while they hovered over the keyboard. I quickly double checked that the Obol coins were still in my back pocket. Yes, of course they were. I breathed in for five seconds, held it for five seconds, then released it. I calmly typed…

...The Watcher didn't need gateways to access her own domain; she herself was the gateway. She walked along the river Styx bank, marvelling at the sights and sounds. The sun that neither set nor rose warmed her skin.

The gravel under her shoes lightly crunched, getting the attention of the one she sought.

Varik.

He had been sitting on the bank, looking out over the river. He jumped to his feet.

"Who are you?" he sneered.

"The Watcher," she said.

"Ah, I have been told about you. You are a human, are you not?" He looked at her in disbelief, betraying his cocky tone.

His tattered clothes were a contradiction to his handsome form. His black hair fell freely into his sharp green eyes, his lips a noticeable contrast to his pale skin.

"A female came here looking for her home. Where has she gone?"

"I don't answer to humans. I do feed from them though." He smirked, then revealed his teeth. He took two steps towards her.

The Watcher held her hand out, palm up, then rose him off the floor. "I could snap every bone in your body," she threatened without a trace of malice. She didn't want to hurt him.

"What are you?" he shouted, kicking his legs out.

"The female that came here, where is she?"

"That mad female accused me of losing the kingdom. I almost lost my head when she flew into rage. She rambled on about her beloved father and ash, you, the Watcher. I don't know where she went," he answered honestly.

The Watcher knew this wasn't going to be easy. She lowered him back to the ground.

"Your information will be rewarded." The Watcher reached into her pocket, then showed him the two coins.

He rushed forward but didn't get very far. The Watcher took him off his feet again.

"She could be the only female left. Why would I tell you anything?" he said aggressively.

The Watcher held up the coins, and he gave up struggling against her hold.

"She was mad, as I said. She did know who I was though, and our history." He shook his head as if trying to remember. "She hated you, told me she would kill your father and male."

So, she did plan to kill the Watcher's male. This would not happen.

"Continue."

"She went back through the gateway. That's all I know."

Ivy would have had two coins. The Watcher wondered why she hadn't given Varik the other one. Perhaps it was to punish him.

"Did she say where she would be staying in the human realm?"

Varik frowned. He was desperate for those coins;

he couldn't stay trapped here in isolation for a day longer. He tried to recall what the mad vampire had said.

"She spoke about living in your home without detection."

That must have been her time in Gary's home.

"Continue," the Watcher barked.

"She met you on a bridge... a bridge next to your home. She said she would return to the bridge to watch you."

Realisation came to the Watcher. It was dark under the bridge; it would have protected her from the sun.

The Watcher lowered Varik to the floor. She flipped one coin to him. He caught it, holding it in his hand like a baby bird.

"There is something I want to show you before I leave." The Watcher grinned. "Goodboy, Goodboy," she called out.

"If you hurt him, Watcher, you will die," he hissed.

This pleased the Watcher.

Goodboy manifested from behind the Watcher, then galloped towards Varik. He looked at him, then back at the Watcher. He cocked his head, confusion dancing in his eyes. He then bounced back over to the Watcher.

"Stay away, Goodboy," Varik warned.

Not knowing what the Watcher was or what she was capable of, he stepped forward to protect his dog. She raised her palm in warning.

"Believe it or not, I've known him a lot longer than you have. I gave him to you, to protect, and you did," she smiled, while Goodboy nuzzled her hand.

"What are you, really?"

"I told you." She flipped the second coin to him. "Enjoy your freedom, Varik."

The Watcher casually turned back in the direction she'd come from. As she walked along the bank, she levitated small stones using her new gift. She smiled secretly to herself...

The sun shone through my window into my eyes, pulling me out of my trance. I scrolled up, wanting to reread what I had written, but my eyes were heavy. I rubbed my back pocket and reached inside to double check. I smiled to myself; the coins were gone. It worked.

I was up and would stay up and wait for Bowen to come back. Not that I could sleep now, not knowing what I knew. I made myself a coffee and stood at my window like I'd done a thousand times, but this time it was different. The bridge that was always in the background while I watched the ducks was now the centre of attention. It was a beautiful stone structure that was not in keeping with the flats that surrounded it. I hadn't noticed that before. The river's banks ran underneath the bridge. I could only see one side from my view. My guess was that Ivy was staying on the other side, out of view.

This was the longest I'd been from Bowen in a while, and I already missed him, worried for him. Plus, I needed to tell him where Ivy was. We needed to end this. I checked the time on my phone, only to realise it had run out of battery again. Oh shit. I quickly turned on the TV to get the time. Adverts, more shitty adverts, come on, come on. Finally, they ended. Seven thirty. My blood ran cold.

Over and over, I recalled what he said. No later than six fifteen; or did he say seven fifteen? No, he didn't, and even if he did, he'd still be late. Any other time would have been fine. I knew he often had breakfast somewhere with his colleagues after a night shift. But he wouldn't have done that this morning. I tried to convince myself that maybe he did, that he'd tried to ring me but my phone was off.

I looked back over to the bridge.

If that bitch had hurt him, I'd kill her, then I'd bring her back along with her family, and then kill them again, this time in front of her.

This was my story, and I was taking it back.

***

I headed straight to the river's bank that was out of my window's view. I trod carefully down, quietly. But I already knew she could hear me.

"Come down, Watcher, or I will snap his neck."

"Stay back, Zoe," Bowen called out.

Then I heard him yelp. I slid down the rest of the bank and came to an abrupt stop.

His handsome face was screwed up in agony, while Ivy stood behind him, both hands splayed either side of his head. He was still in uniform and was sat on the bank, one leg facing forward, the other bent back at an awkward angle. It was broken. The bone protruding from the black fabric made me light-headed. I was going to pass out. No, please no. I just needed to breathe.

"Let him go." My voice trembled.

"I think not," Ivy smirked. "I want answers."

Umbra walked around Ivy, hissing. Wretched cat.

"Zoe, please go back."

Ivy whipped his head to the side, enough to hurt him,

but not enough to kill him, then forced his head upwards, facing him to her. "Do not speak."

"Don't hurt him. I took your father and then you took mine. We're even."

"Are we? You destroyed my kingdom, and I want to know how you did it."

Knowing that she wouldn't be satisfied with my answer, I started to tell everything from start to finish. At first, she looked at me as if I were mad, then she lost patience.

"Liar," she bellowed. "No human has that power."

"Think about it. What did your bedroom look like? What did the landscape look like surrounding your castle? What did your castle look like? You don't know because I hadn't described it in my story."

I can see her thinking this through, wanting to ask me more. I continued. "This is the first time you have been to the human world, because you were born in my story's time frame. Your people have never been here because I started the story while you were all trapped."

"Impossible. My father," she choked. "My father has told me much of the human world."

"Because that's how I created him. I gave him memories of a world he had never known. I needed to give you all a reason to want to escape. He has never left the Inner Temple."

She thought this through. She was about to say something, then didn't. I saw unshed tears in her eyes, then I noticed the rest of her. Her cloak was covered in mud, her face gaunt, her hair like mine, unbrushed. She was in mourning, like me.

"I have the power to restore your kingdom, bring back your family," I offered with very little choice.

She smirked at me; all traces of vulnerability gone. "You're just a human. Why do you think you have that power?"

I held my palm up, then faced it to her, hoping this would work. What felt like pins and needles travelled down my arm to my open hand. If I could just push her back away from Bowen, I might have a chance.

Ivy looked at my open hand, then cocked her head. Umbra hissed. She tightened her grip on Bowen, making him yelp out again. Sweat poured from his temples. He looked like he was about to pass out, and I wanted him to. I couldn't bear to see him in pain.

"Are you a witch, Watcher? I think not." She looked uneasy now.

"Why won't you accept my offer?"

"Accept it, only for you to delete us, as you put it?" Her eyes flared with anger.

"You will have my word," I lied, and she knew it.

Could I snap the bones in her fingers quick enough, and risk Bowen? I was running out of options.

"This feels like a game of chess, does it not?"

Chess? She thought this felt like a game of chess. She was always a few moves ahead, but she never won. Why didn't she win? Because she only focused on her father's moves before he closed in, always giving up before checkmate. A memory of David teaching me how to play flickered through my mind. He always reprimanded me for defending and never attacking. "You'll never win if you don't attack. And don't just focus on my next moves, plan your own," he'd said.

"Tell me what you want," I said, ignoring her.

"I want you to watch your male die," she said coldly, then breathed in his scent from the top of his head.

She wanted a reaction from me, to detect my next move.

Was there shock on her face when she said Goodboy would starve, and I said I didn't care? I thought so.

I looked down at Bowen. "It's over for the time being, my love, but that's okay, I'll bring you back," I said without emotion. Bowen's eyes widened. On the inside I cried. I turned to leave.

"Do not turn your back on me," she bellowed, releasing Bowen.

I ignored her, then called out, "Goodboy, Goodboy."

The splashing to my right confirmed his arrival. Ivy screamed with anger. Her hands fisted to her sides.

"You remember Goodboy, don't you?" I goaded.

I've got you, bitch. Power surged once again down my arm, but this time I kept it to my side.

Goodboy whined and bounded over to Bowen, sniffed at his broken leg, then howled. He was no longer the dog that was humiliated for amusement. He was strong, powerful and above all, he was loyal.

"Goodboy," Bowen breathed.

"I was right, he is your familiar," she said smoothly, but her hands trembled. She stepped into the shallow water. "Perhaps I will take your offer, Watcher."

When I made no move to answer, she took another step. She was getting ready to run, but where? The sun was up. She had nowhere to go. I smirked.

Both Goodboy and I stepped into the water to circle her. Goodboy snapped his jaws at her, making her step towards me. I lifted my hand, palm facing her, making her step backward. Goodboy's menacing growls echoed under the bridge. His heckles rose; he looked demonic.

"As I said, I will take your offer," she trembled.

"The offer has expired."

With no moves left to make, she rushed at me. Her teeth almost made contact with my neck when I let my power surge to push her back. She flew over Goodboy, hitting her head on the bank. She screamed in defiance and rushed at me again. She was too quick for me this time and I was unable to concentrate and bring forth my new power.

This time she made contact. My shoulder stung under her bite, then her head snapped back. I fell back into the water and used my elbows to right myself. Blood poured down my arm, but I couldn't feel anything. When I stood, I was stunned. What looked like a shark attack in the shallow water was Goodboy with her head in his mouth. He thrashed his head from side to side. Ivy's body, like a rag doll, complied.

"That's my boy, Goodboy," I heard Bowen whisper.

I wanted to run to him, but I needed to help Goodboy finish this. I waded through the water and tried to grip on to her ankles, but she managed to kick me back. Enough. I leapt back up then climbed on to her body. I positioned my knees on her chest. Umbra jumped on my bloodied shoulder, hissing and clawing at my neck. To hurt me, she had to become tangible. I grabbed her and threw her off.

Goodboy let go but only to regrip his jaws around her throat. I reached around my back and pulled my knife out from my pocket. It was the original knife I was going to use in the first place. Not so useless now.

The skin on Ivy's neck started to stretch and tear. Blood darkened the water. I held my knife to her neck, unable to use it. Her eyes were wide with terror, my eyes in her face. She thrashed in a last bid to buck me off, but it spurred Goodboy on. He growled loud in defiance and pulled back.

"No—" was her last word.

Umbra, knowing this was over, darted away.

My knees were still on her chest when her head ripped free, her blood now flowing down the river. Her body then started to deflate and decompose beneath me. That too flowed down the river.

"Zoe."

I crawled over to Bowen and knelt behind him so that he could lean back on me. "What do I, what do I?"

"My radio. She chucked it over there." He pointed in the direction.

I slowly moved out of the way and laid him back. I looked back at Goodboy. He was playing with what was left of Ivy's head. Don't look. I desperately fanned back the reeds. Where was it? I couldn't find it.

"Your phone?" I called back.

"Broken."

I found what I thought was his radio, but it was his taser. He must have put up a fight. I couldn't think about that now. Found it. I rushed back over and handed it to him.

"I'm going to tell them I fell in after Missy. Okay?" He smiled through his pain.

"What happened? How did she get you down here—"

"When I got home. At the front door. Still dark." He gritted his teeth.

"I'm sorry."

"Not your fault. It's over now."

"It's over." I smiled at him while stroking his hair back from his face. He gave me a tight-lipped smile then he called it in. He was right; it was over. This chapter, this story, was over, but really it was just the beginning.

CHAPTER 15

My mind often wandered back to Ivy. I hadn't slept well after her death. Was it her fault that she retaliated? No, it was all on me. While I was packing up the flat, I couldn't stop thinking about her, what she'd been through, her heartbreak, her fears. I went back to the riverbank where she had waited, watched, and found her bag.

I wept while I pulled out her belongings. The phone and sunglasses had been crushed; the money ripped up. She would have been bewildered, scared, just as I had wanted. But instead of going back to her kingdom, she stayed. Her desire to free her people overrode her misplacement. Would I have done the same if I were her? Yeah, I would have.

The last item in her bag was the photo of her mother and father, just as I imagined they would look. She killed David because I killed her father; if she had killed David first, I would have killed hers. We were the same. Did I, in some way, kill myself? No, just a part of myself died with her.

I needed to take responsibility for my actions. At the time, I wasn't sure of the possibilities. Releasing a vampire to off the neighbours was just a chance I took, wishful thinking, but the intent was there. I wanted them gone, not just from my building, but from the face of the earth.

"Zoe? Hello."

"Er… sorry." I blushed. "I still have a lot on my mind."

"That's understandable. Okay. So, Zoe, we're coming to the end of our session, is there anything specific you wanted to discuss? Or anything that stood out to you?"

I used to hate this part of the session because I could never think of anything to say. I used to just repeat my weekly response.

"I think you were definitely right, I was under a lot of stress, still am." My thoughts turned to David. "Being busy, moving, being at the hospital with Bowen and trying to keep the shop open has been stressful, but… I don't know, maybe it's taken my mind off it a little."

"How about when you're no longer busy?" Lucy asked.

"I don't know," I answered honestly.

"We will discuss that when the time comes. Have you been sleeping?"

"Not at first. I have been this week, though. It's helped me stay focused."

"That's good." She gave me an encouraging smile. "Have you been writing?"

"No. I think I'll just stick to reading," I lied.

***

Bowen shook his head at me furiously. He was going to give me one hell of a bollocking when we got home.

"Lovely send off, poppet."

"Thank you, but it was Sally and Bowen who organised it," I whispered, not caring that people saw me talking to myself.

They probably wondered why I wasn't crying too, but I didn't care.

David looked over to Bowen and mouthed, "Thank you."

Bowen nodded to him then used his crutches to shuffle closer to me. "Really?" he snapped.

Sally frowned at him.

He looked straight ahead, shook his head again, then looked back down at David's coffin. He was not happy.

"I didn't tell him that you were coming." I blushed, glancing back at Bowen.

"I couldn't miss my own funeral, could I? I always wondered who'd turn up." He looked around, impressed with the turnout, his new green eyes shining with pride.

When Missy first saw him walking through the headstones, she peed in excitement. She and Goodboy ran right over to him. But this wasn't the first time I had seen David. I waited for him in his shop, shortly after Bowen and I moved into his home. My top-floor flat was no good for him while he recovered. I was stacking books not long after I had finished his story, when I'd heard him call out my name. He was sitting behind his desk, grinning. He stood up as he always had and hugged me. "I'm sorry," I'd sobbed into his shoulder. "Don't be sorry. I'm not." He'd let me go to look around his shop. "Oi, are they my books from my home?"

Smiling at that memory earned me a few frowns as I stepped forward to throw dirt on his coffin. I couldn't just bring David back from the dead; it wouldn't have been accurate. Plus, too many people knew he had died. Having his ghost with me, or my version of a ghost, was more than enough.

Then the time came to thank everyone for coming. Sally hugged me and told me she needed to go and let the caterers in. The wake was taking place in his shop, but us three would be running late.

"Really, Zoe?" Bowen fumed.

I went over and wrapped my arms around his waist, careful not to knock his crutches. The graveyard wasn't wheelchair friendly, but he insisted he came, and was now struggling.

"I wanted to tell you, but you've had to deal with so much already."

It was true. While we were in the hospital waiting for his X-ray, he asked me how I was able to send Ivy flying across the river without touching her.

Instead of telling him, I showed him. I took his hand and placed a two-pence coin in it. I looked around to double-check we were alone, then raised it, letting it hover between our hands. He looked sick, so I made a mental note to never use my telekinesis ability in front of him again. At least not until he asked.

"I told you to tell me everything, no more surprises."

"You're right, I'm sorry."

David walked away with the dogs to give us some space.

"If I'm completely honest, I've only written about him in his shop, and only added him to his funeral this morning because he wanted to come. We weren't sure if it would work," I said quietly. I was still getting used to it myself, still exploring the possibilities. Luckily, I had David back to help me.

I looked down, gutted that I'd hurt him.

He ran his fingers through my hair. "Okay, but tell me what you're planning next time."

"I will," I promised.

He was right, I should share everything with him, and that included Varik. While Bowen was resting one evening, I took the dogs for a walk. They were both racing towards the ball that they never brought back, when Goodboy darted across the field into the darkness. I looked up to see Varik watching us.

After he greeted our shared dog, he cautiously made his way to me. "Watcher." He ran a hand through his hair. "The world has changed much," he'd started. "I suppose it has to you, although technically this is the first time you have been in the human realm." I had smiled at him, letting him know that I wasn't a threat. He'd frowned and said, "Impossible. I have memories." I hadn't wanted to hurt him, but I had to answer honestly. "Because… I gave them to you. I can help you, if you'll let me."

I should have told Bowen, but I really was worried about the amount he had to deal with, and selfishly I was scared of losing him.

"What are you thinking about?" he asked, shuffling on his crutches.

"Varik's in Witney." I waited for his rightful anger towards me, but it never came.

"Okay," he said slowly. "Do we need to kill him?"

We both looked over at Goodboy.

"No. I need to take responsibility for my creations. Amber Morris is my responsibility too. Can you accept that?" I asked, looking down at the grass again.

"Goodboy would have been scared coming back into the world for the first time. Maybe he thought Amber was chasing him while she was jogging. We'll never know. You need to remember why you resurrected him in the first place."

"I do. But—"

"And he hasn't hurt anyone else since. Has he?"

Well, he had. But if he hadn't then Bowen wouldn't be here with me.

"Bowen, please. I'm not faultless."

"No, you're not. But you didn't know the full impact of your abilities. You do now." He said 'abilities' slowly, not knowing what else to call it.

I nodded, keeping my eyes down. Maybe he was right. However, I would be writing with caution. No more mistakes.

He hobbled closer to curl a finger under my chin, lifting my face to his. "Let's walk back to the shop, get this over and done with."

"I'll get your wheelchair. Can you make it to the gate?" I smiled. He returned it, then kissed me.

"Yeah, I'll make it."

While we made our way back, we discussed the plesiosaurs.

"When my leg heals, we'll go north. We need to help them, using your… your, well, you know."

"Abilities?"

"Yeah," he smirked, then looked up, smiling adoringly at me.

Bowen and I had been heartbroken when the first two had been caught for 'research' purposes. The world divided on it. Some wanted them captured to study them up close; the environmentalists argued that they could only be studied in their natural habitat.

"I'd like to offer my assistance. I made it here, I will be able to travel further," David said.

"Of course," Bowen said. He looked amused while watching David waving his hands in people's faces as they walked past. We really were new to this.

Bowen also wanted me to write Harry into existence, to lead the anti-poaching force against the hunters. He wanted me to create a ship that sonar couldn't detect, and that could disappear into the mists without a trace. He wanted a ghost ship and a crew that could handle the supernatural.

For Bowen, I would do anything.

With caution.

BOWEN

Ten months later

My hands were always frozen. I rubbed them together then blew my hot breath into them. Nothing worked. It was my fault for losing my gloves again. I held on to the railing, starboard side to get a better look. It was early morning and the sun still hadn't risen, but I could still see a ship in the distance.

"What do you think, friend or foe?"

"I don't know, you've got the binoculars," I snapped.

"It's hard to tell, no markings, no flag either. I hope it's poachers. I'm bloody starving."

"Let me see." I snatched my night vision binoculars back from Varik.

I wasn't happy about Varik joining our crew, but it was what Zoe wanted. Thinking about her made my heart quicken. It had been three months since I'd last seen her, and although we spoke every day on the phone, I missed her.

"You're in luck. I see a harpoon."

"Yes! I'll inform Captain Harry," he said excitedly, then clapped his hands for Goodboy to follow.

Varik wasn't fond of sharing our dog, and that was fine. He could behave like a child sometimes, so I had to pick my battles with him. Watching him drink from one of the poachers when they boarded our ship made me puke all over my boots. He laughed, called me a pussy then smiled, revealing his bloodied sharp teeth. I should have felt horrified by his actions, and I did, but the truth was, that poacher was holding a gun to my head. Varik saved my life. I told him not to tell Zoe, but of course as soon as the words left my mouth, he rang her, he told her. Not forgetting to mention I had puked.

I allowed my thoughts to return to Zoe, remembering when I'd first seen her. It was at Rob's. I was sitting in the waiting area, watching her cut. I couldn't take my eyes off her. Then we got a call out to a suspected dog attack. She was so desperate to save Goodboy. It had warmed me, making me remember something my grandma used to say. "Never trust a girl who doesn't like animals." After that I was desperate to get to know her. I could tell she wasn't anything like my past girlfriends; she was different. She was beautiful, but shy, unsure of herself. When I was asking her out, I had to think fast; she didn't socialise like most others. Museums were quiet and humble, like her. I took a gamble and won. Although she'd become very confident in the last few months, her humbleness still remained.

I wanted to phone her now, to hear her voice, but she'd still be working at this time. She was happy working in David's shop and that was why I didn't push too hard for her to come with me. Although I was glad now, three months, one week, two days and seven hours aboard the *AmberIvy* was too long. Every day felt like a week.

Two weeks into our mission, we witnessed a plesiosaur being captured and killed. Staring into my girlfriend's eyes set into the face of that beautiful creature while it died, changed me. Another reason why I was glad she hadn't come. She already had the weight of the world on her shoulders.

I looked forward to the crew rotation that was in three weeks. Some, like David and Goodboy could come and go as they pleased. Sometimes I wished I had that ability, but I would never say it out loud, especially not to Zoe. Still, it would be interesting to meet our new additions, to see what she had created.

There was a lot more work left that needed to be done. The plesiosaurs were breeding now and if they kept on getting captured, they'd be bred in captivity. But I needed a break. I needed to be with her.

I needed some normality back, I thought, then smiled to myself. My life would never be normal again, because when I got back, I planned on asking the Watcher to marry me.

ACKNOWLEDGEMENTS

I would like to thank Mike, who has supported me from the very start, Mark Warrick, who corrected my many bloopers (muzzle, not snout) and helped me delve deeper into our own town's myths and legends. I would also like to thank David Hill, who brought the Hellfire Caves map to life, and Troubador publishing for all their hard work and patience. I really hope I have done Witney proud, if not, I will go into hiding.

ABOUT THE AUTHOR

Kelly Barker was born in Oxford and moved to Witney ten years ago for work. She has been a barber since 2002, and loves her job. The protagonist of her debut novel, *The Inner Temple*, is also a barber. She has had many authors in her chair over the years, and has been inspired by them all.

Next book by Kelly Barker...

Even The Gods Fear It

Zoe is torn between her new-found abilities, to create characters into existence through her storytelling, and her loved ones. Her fiancé Bowen wants to protect her, but she feels as though she can't breathe.

When Bowen sets sail, taking one last trip in a desperate bid to save the plesiosaurs from extinction, she and Varik, one of her creations, release something so deadly it was rumoured that even the gods feared it.

She is now faced with two choices. With the world divided over her creations, the line between right and wrong have blurred. Will Zoe finally understand that you can't have all that power without any repercussions, or will she destroy herself in the process?

This book is printed on paper from sustainable sources managed under the Forest Stewardship Council (FSC) scheme.

It has been printed in the UK to reduce transportation miles and their impact upon the environment.

For every new title that Matador publishes, we plant a tree to offset CO_2, partnering with the More Trees scheme.

For more about how Matador offsets its environmental impact, see www.troubador.co.uk/about/